TITANIS

I loved this story! A handsome, heartbreaking hero fighting his demons; a courageous, compassionate heroine who possesses the key to unlock the past—and set him free. Set on the beautiful seas off Australia's coast, Titanis is a fast-paced, romantic, poignant adventure—the perfect *Saturday* afternoon read! I promise, you won't be disappointed!

—**Susan May Warren, admitted Ronie Kendig fan and USA Today best-selling, RITA award-winning author of *Wild Montana Skies***

Ronie Kendig brings her trademark action and adventure Down Under as she treats readers to a story they have been clamouring for – that of Australian SAS soldier, Eamon "Titanis" Straider, left reeling at the close of *Falcon*. Plunging Eamon, his crew, and unwanted guests aboard his super yacht into a whirlwind of danger, Kendig ups the ante as a man with a vendetta and a woman hiding lifelong secrets bring Titanis to his knees. Kendig's unique talent for hair-raising action scenes and sizzling romantic tension is once again on display in this brilliantly executed romantic thriller.

—**Rel Mollet, RelzReviewz.com**

Secrets, romance, tension, and heart-pounding action set against the backdrop of a stunning Australian landscape. *Titanis* is a wild and passionate ride you won't soon forget.

—**Emilie Hendryx of Thinking Thoughts Blog**

He's back! *Titanis* is full of brilliant writing, emotional and romantic tension, and in true Ronie Kendig-fashion, rapid-fire action. We've been clamoring for Titanis's story, and Ronie doesn't disappoint! A perfect fit into The Quiet Professionals series, I am *so* excited to see this bit of perfection come to life!

—**Mikal Dawn, author of the debut novel, *Count Me In***

Wow! Ronie Kendig does NOT disappoint in this novella featuring the brooding, Aussie hero, Eamon "Titanis" Straider! A nonstop voyage from the first line to the last scene, this story will leave you breathless and wanting to read it again and again!!

—**Steffani Webb, book reviewer and owner of The Cozy Life Shop (Etsy)**

TITANIS

THE QUIET PROFESSIONALS | A NOVELLA

RONIE KENDIG

ALSO BY RONIE KENDIG

THE QUIET PROFESSIONALS
RAPTOR 6
HAWK
FALCON

THE TOX FILES
THE WARRIOR'S SEAL
CONSPIRACY OF SILENCE
CROWN OF SOULS (SEP 2017)

THE DISCARDED HEROES
NIGHTSHADE
DIGITALIS
WOLFSBANE
FIRETHORN

A BREED APART
TRINITY
TALON
BEOWULF

STANDALONE TITLES

OPERATION ZULU: REDEMPTION

DEAD RECKONING

Titanis
© 2017 by Ronie Kendig
Print Edition
ISBN 978-0-9981367-1-4

All rights reserved. No part of this publication may be reproduced or transmitted in any form or by any means without written permission of the publisher.

This book is a work of fiction. Names, characters, places, and incidents are either products of the author's imagination or used fictitiously. Any similarity to actual people, organizations, and/or events is purely coincidental.

Cover design by Emilie Hendryx of E.A. Creative Design

Author is represented by Steve Laube of the Steve Laube Agency

They shall grow not old, as we that are left grow old:
Age shall not weary them, nor the years condemn.
At the going down of the sun and in the morning,
We will remember them.

Ode of Remembrance, *For the Fallen*
Laurence Binyon (1914)

CHAPTER 1

ViCross Yacht, Cape York, Australia

THE TERRITORY OF being a soldier came with being assaulted. By the enemy. But when one of your own did the betraying, it carved a cruel mark. Right across his temple and jaw. Even now beneath chlorinated waters, the difference could be felt. In his face. In his life. His heart.

Breath held, Eamon Straider clutched the fifty-pound weight to his chest as he stalked across the bottom of the deep end of the pool. Pushing against the resistance offered by the water and the burden he carried, he was struck by the reality that the weight in his arms wasn't so different from the one in his heart.

With each step, he approached the shallow end until the water reached his eyes.

It was his own fault. Mates died because he couldn't get his head out of the past.

Another push. His nose breached the surface. He refused himself a breath even though it'd been a minute thirty underwater. Refused to give the weight straining against his efforts the pleasure of conquering him. Longer. Better. Stronger. He would beat this. He wouldn't again allow a burden to control him or his life.

His chest pounded from the exertion, echoing its pleas in his temples.

Never again.

She had betrayed him and his mates. And that clung to

him like the water now dripping from his chin. How had he not seen the signs, seen the writing on the proverbial wall? The truth of it was—he had seen it, but he'd ignored the evidence so he could get cozy with her.

He'd taken that broken focus into another mission. It left him with a permanent reminder of his failure. Because of a woman.

Never again.

Eamon set down the weight on floor and placed his palms on the lip of the pool. With care, with focused control, he released his breath. Drew in a long draught of air. Released it. In. Out.

Leaning against the pool lining, he stared down the length, past the elaborate murals of his beloved country that adorned, and straight out to the fourth "wall"—an opening that gave the appearance of the water bleeding into the warm waters of Cape York. Sunlight glared off the ocean.

"*What's the call, Titanis? In or out?*"

"*Give me a sec,*" he'd bit out, studying the readings, both digital and facial. *Was this woman lying? Sending them in to get them killed, the same way Brie had?*

"*If she's wrong, that's fish in a barrel,*" Niehauer said.

Pulse steadied, he turned and lifted the black weight over his head and trudged back toward the deep end, focus singularly honed on strengthening his mind and body. Part of that included isolation for quiet contemplation. Talking to God. He'd never done it enough, and even now wrestled with the Almighty over a few things.

The water rose with his determination to be clear-headed. Focused. Stronger. Better. For himself. For Cory Niehauer. For any mate God might put in his path to protect. To make sure he didn't fail his charge. So he didn't have to attend another funeral evidencing his weakness and failure.

Never again.

Submerged, the weight became that bitter enemy from a

year ago. The house in that village. The bullet that shaved off a year of his life and a section of his beard. Screams. Searing heat. Strafing gunfire. Howls of pain and the dying.

Eamon hesitated, the memories overwhelming. Grief choking.

His lungs writhed for a breath.

An anxious, panicked one.

Brown eyes. Small, firm lips.

The unbidden memory erupted. Lieutenant Brie Hastings had carved that mark on him with her lies, with her willing kisses laced with deception. He'd been the fool eating what she served. *Sap.* He'd been chuffed that she showed interest in him. Chased it. Chased her.

His trust in and blindness to her lies cost lives, even after she'd been long put away in an American federal penitentiary. She'd ruined him. *Destroyed* him.

Eamon held. The weight. The breath. His position.

She swam at him, alluring. Attractive. Intelligent.

"It's you—you're the mole."

Her lip lifted in a sneer. "You have no idea what you're talking about."

Eamon dropped the weight. Surged to the surface. Hauled in a greedy breath then let out a meaty growl that he'd lost focus. Lost control. Hugging the edge of the pool, he worked to steady his ragged breathing. Didn't care about the chlorinated water dripping into his eyes. Trained his gaze on the undulating waters beyond the *ViCross*. The Torres Strait Islands in the far distance.

But not far enough. Way too close to civilization. To people. They'd get even closer with the guests, giving them a tour of the Gulf of Carpentaria.

A black dot hung in the sky. Already? He glanced at the clock on the wall and released another breath. No, not yet. Maybe the last of the staff. His mother wasn't due to arrive with the first wave of dignitaries for another two hours.

Though he resented the invasion of his life and business—his super yacht had become the headquarters for Tri-S, his security firm—he would never turn away family. Even when he knew his mother brought Australia's elite to rub elbows with him and secure another generation of Straiders in power or politics, or both. He'd taken to living on the *ViCross* to limit opportunities for betrayal. Not to cut out his parents. Though, he would admit to stifling their influence in his life as well. Mouth against his crossed arms and cool water lapping at his waist, he eyed the chopper again. The next one would bring the invasion that would demand he once more don civility instead of Kevlar.

"Titanis."

He shot a look over his shoulder. His mate Victor "Thor" Thorsen, a one-time mixed-martial arts fighter and American soldier whom he'd hired for this stint, stood on the other side of the pool. They'd met in Iraq during a tour that cemented their friendship with ammo and eliminating threats. With a kid to feed and wife to look after, Thor needed the money and a week-long endeavor would pay his mortgage for a few months.

Although Thor enjoyed a workout as much as Eamon, they all knew not to interrupt Eamon's time. So there was only one reason he'd come below deck. "Yeh. Saw it." The chopper thundered overhead. "See them to their rooms." The staff had quarters on this deck, just as the captain and crew had quarters on the wheel deck. But he didn't need to be there for staff, though he'd be sure to introduce himself to the newcomers. "I need a few more reps."

"Still don't understand why you okayed this."

"Neither do I," Eamon muttered, then swung around and released the wall, treading water.

"Tariq found some interesting traffic he wants you to see."

Eamon swiped the water from his face. "I'll be up in a few."

"Sounds good." Thor gave a curt nod and exited.

Taking several measuring breaths, Eamon stared at the weight on the pool floor. Then dove in, harnessing his frustration—over Brie, over Niehauer, over the coming invasion of his yacht and life—and lifted the weight. Crossed his arms over his chest and hugged it as he made several more switchbacks. Calming himself. Controlling himself. Forcing himself to stay below water longer. He'd managed to get to three minutes and thirty-two seconds. Anything to prove he could do it. He could conquer it.

Because that failure, that idiocy . . . would not control him. *Never. Again.*

GOD REALLY KNEW how to make a beautiful man. It didn't help that he'd erupted from the pool like an all-powerful god, dripping water and power. Sculpted muscles rippled beneath his left arm that bore an elaborate sleeve tattoo. An inked cross covered his right pectoral. Dark brown hair framed a heavily tanned face with firm planes and raw intensity.

Definitely godlike.

Ellis Rostov-Leclair stood rooted at the bottom of the stairs. When she'd first spied the pool through the glass doors, she thought she'd found a respite from the noise and chatter of the dignitaries, who'd come in on the helicopter with her and Alaina Straider. Never had she imagined a yacht could be this big, and its enormity and luxury had drawn her further into its depths to discover its beauty and mysteries. Why did someone need a pool like this when they were on a yacht? She gave a half laugh.

He snapped his head around. Eyes blue like the water and piercing as Poseidon's trident delivered a fierce glower. Dark brows drew together.

Oh. Ellis fought the urge to spin around and crash back

through the door. *Say something. Anything.*

"Ah, I see you found my son," Alaina said, drifting through the door, then arcing an eyebrow.

Ellis yanked her gaze to her toes as heat rose through her cheeks.

Alaina touched her elbow as she drew alongside. "Honestly, Eamon. Could you not at least be dressed for our arrival? Here you are, practically naked before dear Hayley."

Hating the deception of that name and being caught staring like a wide-eyed guppy, Ellis shifted toward the door. "I . . . I should go . . ."

"Had I known you were coming several hours earlier than agreed, I would have prepared myself." His voice was deep and calm, as the god of the seas should be, but there was an edge, a bite to them, so subtle but definitely there. Water splashed as he climbed out of the pool.

Mercy, the man had definitely worked out. His shoulders V'ed down to a trim waist. Legs were as muscled as the rest of him. She'd watched him push through the water with that weight, amazed. In awe, if she were honest. He made the trek as any other might on a track. With air.

Another tattoo on his shoulder blade rolled as he lifted a towel and faced them. Eamon locked his attention on his mother. "If you will excuse me, I'll make myself more presentable." Those eyes struck Ellis next, and he gave a curt nod of acknowledgement before stalking through the glass doors.

"I upset him," Ellis whispered to herself.

"Everything upsets Eamon these days," Alaina said with a longsuffering sigh. But then she smiled. "He's easy on the eyes, isn't he?"

Heat shot through her face again. "I didn't mean . . . I wasn't—" For pity's sake! "I didn't see him when I first came in. Then he shot up out of the water like a god and—"

"Like a god?" Alaina said with a laugh.

Ellis swallowed hard. Had she said that out loud? "This is a mistake."

"What? You and him?"

"Alaina," Ellis said with a tinge of teasing warning. "You know what I meant. Me being here. The fake name. Hiding why I'm here."

"Nonsense." With perfect complexion and composure, Alaina turned toward the stairs. Though she looked at the doors, it seemed her gaze went much farther. "He would never have let you come if he'd known what we intend."

"Are you so terribly sure this is the right—"

"Absolutely." She whirled back and slid her arm through Ellis's, drawing her out of the pool room. "The thing with my son is knowing what he says with his mouth and what he says with his heart." They climbed the stairs back to the main deck. "That Shrew, who shall never be named by me again, shattered him. He's forsaken the military and his mates, as well as most of civilization. He's been on this ship with those sweaty, bearded men since. I host events just to spend time with him, to force him to remember how to conduct himself in front of others. I'm still surprised he agreed to meet the queen."

"I saw those photos in the news. He dwarfed Her Majesty."

"He did." Alaina's soft laugh carried in the confined space. The woman was a statement in elegance and refinement, not easily ruffled or put off from her goal. "And he uses his size to his advantage, to remind people who exactly is in charge." She motioned to the left as they reached the main deck. Another set of glass doors protected a salon, decorated in lush, calming blues and grays that lured her into its comfort. It seemed to say so much about Eamon, about his character. Calm. Light-hearted.

At least, the Eamon she'd known nearly twenty years ago. And he most certainly had not looked like Poseidon back then.

A freckle-faced, knobby-kneed teen. Lanky. But still very confident. Always confident.

Alaina swung around in front of Ellis. Clasped her left hand between her own. Her gaze fell there. She took a breath, hesitation catching her mouth open. "Trust me in this, okay?" Her eyes—so like Eamon's—rose. "And don't let him scare you."

"Scare me?" Ellis's heart tripped, remembering the urge to flee when he snapped that glare at her in the pool room. "He terrifies me. Some men might make threats. He makes good on them."

"He's good at scaring people. Very good. Especially now—all the better to keep them away." She bounced their hands. "But he needs this." A wavering smile brought thin lines to Alaina's eyes. "And so do you. You deserve it as much as he does. You've worked so hard and"—she heaved a contented sighed—"honestly, you've made me so proud. I want to see this happen for you both."

Though Ellis knew Alaina meant the big announcement, a venture on which she would—her stomach squeezed at the thought—be working very closely now with Eamon, she couldn't help but think Alaina alluded to more than the charity. "What if when he finds out, he hates me? Refuses to—"

"He is thick-headed, but Eamon also has common sense. He'll get it sorted." Cold, manicured hands cupped her face. "And how could he not like you, Ellis?"

After that fierce glare? Quite easily.

CHAPTER 2

A SHOWER AND shave didn't cleanse Eamon of the anger tightening his muscles and mood. After punching in his personal code, he accessed the Command center via the backdoor connecting his office to the central hub below the wheel deck. Jacket draped over his arm, he stepped over the heavy steel hatch, buttoning his cuffs. At the nearest chair, he slung the jacket over its back.

Tariq looked up from his workstation, eyes widening before a smile cut through his face. "Thor, you were right," he called over his shoulder to where Thor stood at the light table. 'Ticked' about covers it."

Eamon threw all his annoyance at the MMA fighter. "You could've warned me."

Giving a lazy shrug, he grinned. "More fun this way. Besides, you said you knew."

"I told you to be specific," Tariq warned.

Enough. Eamon joined the one-time translator-turned-griefer-turned-security expert. "You wanted to show me something?"

"Roger that," Tariq said as he shifted his attention to the bank of monitors and nodded. "Your name's been coming up."

That wasn't unusual. As the son of retired Prime Minister Arthur Straider, a fixture of power and influence among Australia's most elite, Eamon had been hounded by journalists and graced—ungraced?—more covers than he'd care to admit. Another reason he'd removed himself to the *ViCross* after Brie and Niehauer.

But Tariq must have something more significant to bring it up. "How so?" He palmed Tariq's desk and leaned in.

"It seems ambiguous enough—a mention of the yacht. A mention of you." Part of his job with Tri-S required Tariq to watch for any threat or invasion of privacy against Eamon and the company itself. He didn't need any more journos pursuing him, and after a tragedy from his childhood that left a little girl dead, Eamon monitored his parents' safety as well, to ensure nobody was used against his father or some other political figure ever again.

"So . . . ?"

Tariq pulled up a file. "I found this on a back-room server."

Those muscles tightened more as Eamon stared at the PDF file—the official invitation to this weekend's event aboard the *ViCross*.

"Someone's inviting himself—"

"—or herself." Pretty green eyes flashed in his mind.

"—to the party." Tariq angled away, disapproval flashing through his expression. "You *cannot* believe she's behind this."

"He doesn't," Thor put in, standing behind them. "He'll do anything to classify her a threat, so he can remove or exclude her."

Eamon straightened. "The fact that there wasn't a twenty-something coed on the approved list has nothing to do with me. All threats need to be assessed, no matter how pretty."

"Well, at least you'll admit she's pretty, but coed?" Thor grunted. "Did we see the same woman? That is not a coed. She's a lady."

"I don't care who she is. I didn't approve her and had no foreknowledge that she was coming."

Hesitant, Tariq lifted a finger. "Um, but Lady Alaina did."

"Don't be so pretentious. Call her Alaina." Eamon

tightened his jaw. "And I'll take it up with her."

"You call it pretension, I call it showing your mom respect, because hello? I do not want to be the wrong side of the formidable Alaina Straider. So go ahead and try," Tariq said, "but when I tried to tell her you wouldn't like this, she said it was her event and this"—he scuttled some papers and lifted a sheet, scanned it, and stabbed a name—"Hayley Warren was coming regardless. And she was to have a VIP suite."

VIP. Why was she that important to his mother? "Who got displaced to a bunk?"

"That too was Alaina's doing—she said to move Barton."

Shaking his head, he could only imagine the rumors that would fly over him placing a member of Parliament in a room with twin beds. What was to be said of a man whose mother overrode his orders on his own ship? "I'll deal with it."

"And by deal with it," Tariq added with a snicker, "you mean give her a piece of your mind then work to avoid the Miss Warren for the rest of the voyage, because we all know you won't throw a woman overboard like you did that journo."

"That was one time," Eamon groused. The idiot had sneaked aboard to take pictures and Eamon threw him off. Quite literally. Earning himself the nickname the "Beast of Cape York." He stalked to his station and flicked on his monitor. "Who else came in on that bird?"

"Your mother, Ms. Warren, Senator Barton, the Honorable Reginald Haworth and the Honorable Carrington Smith, and a few serving staff. We have another inbound with caterers, and later tonight most of the guests."

His father would arrive just before the party, having no time for 'frivolity,' as he called it. Neither did Eamon, but he would not refuse his mother. Eamon fisted a hand. The ship's complement of ten was about to climb to thirty in order to accommodate the guests his mother insisted upon for this event.

Inwardly, he groaned. Thor was right. He wouldn't remove the girl, but he would have a talk with his mum.

A vibrating noise wormed through the air. Eamon glanced around. "What is that?"

"New phone," Tariq said lifting a small black device. "Sorry."

Coming up out of the water and finding her staring down at him had startled Eamon at first. His crew knew not to bother him down there. But then to see those eyes widen. The pink that rushed into cheeks—it'd set him off. Angered him. What was she doing that far down in the ship? What if this girl was the one who'd forged her way onto the *ViCross*? It was hard to believe—his mum vouched for her and his mother was not easily conned. But then, Eamon thought he'd been pretty sharp about reading people and Brie had gotten past him.

Never again.

"Check that girl," Eamon said, rifling through a stack of papers.

"What"—Tariq tensed when Eamon glared at him—"do you mean?" he switched tones and questions. Cleared his throat. "Mrs. Straider gave me her info. It's there with the others. Put it on your desk last night when she called. Knowing you wouldn't be satisfied with that, I ran her." Tariq bounced his shoulders again. "She's clear, boss. Twenty-six."

Two years older than Eamon would've guessed. What was her connection to his mum? "Education?"

"Honor student. Dean's list. Masters in international business—graduated two years ago from Oxford."

"British then." Maybe that was the problem.

"I guess?" Tariq's voice pitched. "Dude. Are you really that paranoid?"

"She wandered my ship—down to the pool deck. Why? What was she looking for? Recon? Scoping it out before someone else comes?"

Tariq laughed.

Eamon scowled. Why was Tariq blowing her off? He glanced at Thor, who seemed to have a decent appreciation of the situation. "Takes one pretty face to leave a dozen soldiers in a fight for their lives."

"I'm getting that part where you think she's pretty, but a threat?" Uncertainty shaded Tariq's features.

Eamon twitched at the realization he'd twice said she was pretty. "Calling it like I see it."

He swept over the limited profile with her photo. Long reddish-blond hair framed a round face. Blue-green eyes. Born in Melbourne. Went abroad for college. Returned and worked with a charity. How could she afford to work for a charity and still support herself? That peach suit she'd worn was silk, wasn't it? "Run her," he said, nodding toward the computers. "I want more. Financials. Family. Find out her favorite color." He pointed a finger. "I want to know what her connection to my mother is."

Awkward silence settled over the Command deck, grating on his nerves as he felt Thor and Tariq's questioning gazes.

Thor shifted. "Maybe you need another swim to work off that agitation before you go to the dining room."

Eamon nearly cursed as he checked his watch. Already that time. "What I need is my mother to follow the simple rules of conduct on my ship." He flicked a hand at both men. "Get dressed. If I have to endure this dinner, so do you."

Thor barked a laugh that followed Eamon out the door, making him all the more determined to get this—and his mum's disrespect of him—in hand.

"I TALKED WITH the agent today, and it's all set."

Ellis's heart thumped, elation speeding through her veins, followed quickly by a knot of dread. "So, just his signature—

which is part of the ceremony here—and it's done?"

"Only that," Mr. Haworth said with a nod. "I'm very impressed with what you've accomplished, Miss Warren. In fact, so impressed that I would like to talk with you about another venture."

"Thank you, but until the complex is up and running, that's where my attention and heart will be devoted," she said, annoyed that she'd not been able to accomplish this without the veil of deception that had taken over her life as a little girl. "It's been a long journey, but one he and I both believe in."

"Therein lies the irony, yes? He is committed to this and doesn't even know who's behind it, eh?" The man had a nice chuckle, but it made Ellis nervous.

"Whether by one name or another, it's still me." She just hoped—desperately—that Eamon would understand.

"All this time," Haworth said with a laugh in his voice, "and this formidable commando has no idea."

"Please," Ellis said, unsettled at the unspoken insinuation, "give care, Mr. Haworth. I trusted you with a secret, one I'm not particularly proud of, in the hopes we could focus on the goal, on what is being accomplished for our veterans."

Mr. Haworth held up a hand, bobbing his head as if to reassure her all was well. "I worry for you, *Miss Warren*."

Senator Barton gave a grunt, his expression grave. "Straider is not a forgiving man."

"As we are well aware," Haworth agreed.

Barton went on. "If he doesn't understand the asset you are, then we will simply make sure he comes to that understanding."

Haworth shifted as they stood just inside the dining hall. "Eamon's a level-headed businessman, so—"

"Pleased to hear you think so," a deep voice snapped into their conversation, bringing with it the very tall, very commanding Eamon Straider.

Ellis took a step back, heart pounding, realizing their

mistake of having that conversation so close to the door. What had he heard? She watched as the men shook hands.

"Welcome aboard the *ViCross*, Mr. Haworth, Senator Barton," Eamon said, greeting the men. "Sorry I didn't deliver that welcome when you first arrived."

"I told Alaina that we should wait and not arrive early. I know the intricacies that go into preparing for arrivals," Haworth said with a chuckle. "But there is no changing her mind when she's set on something."

"Eamon, m'boy," Senator Barton said, joining them and providing the perfect distraction for Ellis to slip away. "How're the injuries?" Once an SAS soldier himself, Senator Barton had no compunctions against bringing up the scar gouged into Eamon's face. The news had carried for weeks about his near-death experience, the death of his mates. He'd vanished from the limelight after that.

And really, the scar wasn't terrible. In fact, she hadn't even noticed it at the pool with the ocean backlighting him. The flesh of the scar held a pinkish tinge against his heavily tanned face and around his jaw where the tissue interrupted the shadow of his beard. But she'd somehow imagined it to be far more terrible with the way he'd gone into hiding.

The scar wasn't entirely distracting. No, what was distracting was *him*. And those abs . . . biceps . . . blue eyes that felt more like surgeon's hands digging within her brain, probing her secrets. Those eyes . . .

Eyes. *He's looking at me!*

With a start, she straightened. Withdrew her gaze, stomach churning. It'd be one thing if he looked at her with appreciation, but this was a searing, I'm-going-to-figure-out-what-you're-hiding gaze.

Of course, she'd always had an overactive imagination, but this . . . this time it wasn't her OAI. It was him. This wouldn't work. He was far too perceptive. She wove around the room toward Alaina, who was watching closely.

"Better," she heard Eamon finally answer to the senator as she closed the gap between herself and his mother. "Putting it behind me."

Barton clapped Eamon's shoulder. "That's why you're Melbourne's hero."

"How are you?" Alaina whispered, wrapping an arm around her.

Ellis let out a ragged breath. "That was close—Mr. Haworth remarked on how amazed he was that Eamon didn't know who I was, and no sooner had the words left his mouth than Eamon walked in."

For the first time, a glimmer of hesitation appeared in the woman's face as she stared across the room at her son. "Reginald should know better than to mention that. I'll have a word with him." She threaded her arm through Ellis's again. "I'm not going to let anyone ruin this weekend for you. This has been a longtime coming, and Eamon needs it. Whether he knows it or not."

"Knows what?"

Again? Seriously? Ellis's stomach plummeted at the deep rumble of Eamon's voice as he drew alongside them, placed a kiss on his mother's cheek, and planted himself between them.

"Eamon," his mother said in her clipped tone, lifting a glass of lemonade and taking a sip. All grace and elegance. "Nice to see you have clothes on this time."

Ellis adored that Alaina knew how to inject levity into a conversation. But did she have to push the memory of his sculpted chest and biceps into Ellis's mind again?

"You don't play fair, Mum," he teased. His hand slid toward Ellis. "I don't believe we've been introduced. Eamon Straider."

Did he realize he swallowed all breathable air in the room with his enormous presence? And his insistence on being acknowledged—not directly but just this presence he exuded—consumed her field of vision. Heat splashed through her belly as she forced herself to put her hand in his. "El—"

"Hayley Warren meet my overgrown son, Eamon," his mother interrupted Ellis's mistake. "Eamon, Hayley Warren. A very dear girl, instrumental in charitable work. This event is largely her doing."

Ellis bit her tongue, angry at her obvious slip. She hadn't done that in years, but Eamon undid her barriers. Muddled her brain.

His grasp was strong, his gaze digging once more through her secrets, through her lies of the last year. Lies he couldn't know existed, but would soon. And that—that was the reason guilt dripped from her pores.

"That right?" He rubbed his jaw, fingers tracking along the scar, then squared his shoulders. "Helping how?"

"We've worked a few projects," Ellis managed, reminding herself she was a strong, confident woman. "Alaina has been very gracious to take me under her wing and mentor me."

"Yeh? What charities do you favor?"

"Veterans and their families, children—"

"Veterans?" Folding his arms, he seemed to settle in for the conversation and he craned his neck, annoyance glinting. "Why them? Why not low-income?"

Ellis lifted an eyebrow. "That question presumes military families aren't low-income." When his expression didn't change, she forged ahead. "There are many needs and too few resources to assist our veterans."

"Wounded ones?"

That sounded like a challenge, but Ellis refused to be baited. "Not only."

"Surely, if you're so involved in military charities, then you're familiar with Vic Toriael."

Her heart jammed in her throat at the mention of her pseudonym.

"Oh, go and play interrogator with someone else, Eamon. Honestly."

"Just conversation," he insisted, unrelenting, then swung his attention back to Ellis. "Oxford educated."

Ellis somehow felt bare, exposed before him. How in heaven's name had he known about Oxford? "I am." If he knew that . . . it meant he had been digging. Experts had assembled her new identity and history nearly twenty years ago. But he was Eamon . . .

The air felt thin. A throb pulsed at the back of her head.

"Dean's list, as well." His jaw jutted. "Not surprised—my mother is careful about who she lets into her inner circles, Right, Mum?

"You know I am. Unlike you, who lets no one in and interrogates anyone who gets close. You're proud of that Beast of Cape York moniker when you should be ashamed of it." Eamon shrugged. "I didn't create it—"

"But you did, with your gruff manners and perpetual scowl and interrogating"—she waved a hand at Ellis—"poor guests who merely want to enjoy an event."

"Just trying to get to know the people on my boat."

She was thirsty. Felt queasy. Had to get away before he could launch a full inquest.

"Why? Are you that interested in Hayley?" When Alaina gave her an appraising look, Ellis wanted to jump overboard to save Eamon the trouble. "I can understand your interest—she's quite pretty, isn't she? Fair face and figure—"

"Alaina," Ellis breathed around the constriction in her chest and the fire in her cheeks, wishing she could fade from existence.

"Dinner is served," a steward announced.

Thank you, Lord! Saved by the steward. Seizing the distraction, Ellis extricated herself from the humiliating moment and moved toward the long table, bumping into a man looking over his shoulder, laughing.

"Sorry, mate"—his gaze hit hers and widened—"er, ma'am." The Middle Eastern man had dark eyes that brightened with an easy smile. "Miss Warren."

Surprised, she smiled. "Do we know each other?"

Though he'd said "mate," there was nothing Australian about the man with his curly black hair and dark eyes that bespoke his Middle Eastern heritage. "I know everyone onboard." He guided her to the setting with her name on it, then motioned to the other placard. "That's me."

"Tariq Yusef," she said, reading it. "You work here then? Part of the crew, the captain maybe?"

"Not even," he said with a laugh as they sat down. Then he motioned to her other side as an older, burly man assumed the seat. "That's Captain Ezra."

Ellis shared a smile with the captain, who looked like a grizzly in a suit. Dark hair, wiry and almost unkempt. His demeanor was almost as gruff. "So, not the captain. What do you do here?"

"Me?" Tariq shrugged as they took their places, "I work security for Tri-S."

"Straider Security Services," she thought out loud, watching the others fill in the chairs around the table and telling herself not to look at Eamon. But it was hard to ignore Poseidon on his throne. From Alaina's left at the end of the table sat Haworth. No doubt the lady's attempt to keep Mr. Haworth from ruining their endeavor. She didn't recognize the man who sat across from Tariq, but Senator Barton and Mr. Carrington flanked Eamon at the head.

"That's the one. I run everyone's history to vet threats."

Awareness ruptured Ellis's thin hope that she'd survive this meal and the two days before the ceremony without betraying her secret. "So, you would be the reason Eamon knew I was educated at Oxford."

"Afraid so." Tariq leaned closer, his mannerisms light-hearted but also clearly flirtatious. "Don't let the big guy scare you. He's like that—wants everyone off kilter so he can test them, or get rid of them. But he's harmless. Unless you're a terrorist or combatant."

"So the Beast of Cape York doesn't bite?"

Tariq's guffaw echoed around the room, drawing attention. Eamon's attention. "He's sensitive about his privacy. I would be too if my girlfriend nearly got my team killed. He won't let it happen again. Can't blame him really. And I mean, chicks are into him, Beast of Cape York. They all think of themselves as the princess in that yellow dress—what's her name?"

"I don't think she's a princess," Ellis corrected.

Poseidon had once more pinned her beneath his withering gaze, his trident probing the veil of secrecy that had cocooned her life. No matter how handsome, no matter that she had coordinated the entire last two years of her life for him, Ellis knew she had to stay far from Eamon Straider. At least until Sunday. Then . . . then he'd either thank her. Or throw her overboard.

CHAPTER 3

SHE WAS ATTRACTIVE. He'd give his mother that about Hayley Warren. But there was something off about her. And it wasn't her attraction to him, though that was obvious enough with her flushed cheeks each time she found his gaze. Which she did it a lot. Too pretty. Too nervous. Too attentive.

So are you. But he had a purpose, a reason—she was guilty or lying about something.

The buzzing at the back of his brain demanded he continue monitoring her movements. Figure out what she was up to.

She had talked and laughed with Tariq through most of dinner, but as the evening wore on, her ready smile came less readily. She'd barely touched her meal, yet guzzled water. The earlier flush faded, replaced with a telltale blanching. She was probably suffering seasickness. Served her right.

Yet he didn't need someone throwing up and smelling up the *ViCross*. As he listened to Barton and Carrington discuss the relocation of Barton's large plastics factory back to Melbourne, bringing in thousands of jobs once more, Eamon kept an eye and ear on Warren. Plates had been cleared and dessert served, yet still she only picked at her tiramisu. As Tariq assaulted her with his useless flirting, she closed her eyes and swallowed. Hard.

She should've been smart. Quit the dinner and gone to her room to rest. But she pressed on. And that would do her in. She'd need to get above deck. Eye the horizon. But she

remained at his mother's side. As if needing protection.
From me.
The thought annoyed him. Why, he didn't know. It was good that she avoided him. Less chance of him offending his mother's guest, which would surely bring an earful. But he was determined to rout what it was about Warren that had his instincts screaming.

As the meal ended and the guests left the table, he anticipated she'd go above deck. But she didn't. They lingered within the dining room as Haworth and Carrington fell into heavy conversation. Standing near his mother, Warren closed her eyes. Her hand went to her flat stomach. She was about to lose it.

Eamon strode around the guests and came alongside her. Cupped her elbow. Leaned in and said quietly, "Come with me."

She snapped straight, her face draining of what little color she had. Near-white.

He firmed his grip, hating the fear etched into her young face. On a tango, that worked. Served its purpose. On whatever she was, it bugged him.

"Ea—"

He held a silencing hand to his mother as he drew Miss Warren through the doors, not dragging her but also not far from it. If this visit had been about attraction to him, shouldn't she come along more easily? He wouldn't manhandle her, but he also wouldn't let her spew her cookies in front of everyone else.

"Did I do something wrong?"

Man, her voice was soft, plaintive as he guided her to the stairs. "Besides getting sea sick?"

Wide green eyes hit his, as if to ask how he knew. "Where are you taking me?"

"Main deck. Can you walk okay?"

Something shifted in her expression. A strength, a

resilience. "Well enough," she said as they reached the stairs.

Maintaining his hold, he noted how she slowly relied more heavily on his assistance until finally, she hesitated, eyes sliding shut again with a groan.

"I could carry you," he taunted.

"Don't you dare," she growled.

Why it amused him to get a rise out of her, he couldn't say. Besides, if she couldn't handle being aboard without getting sick, she shouldn't be here. One foot hiked on the next step, he rested against the wall, waiting until the wave that turned her complexion green passed. She had a sprinkle of freckles across her nose and cheeks that gave her character.

But he wasn't interested in character. Truth interested him.

"I'm so embarrassed," she whispered, tilting her head against the wall as if she could melt into it.

"Takes time," he forced himself to say. "Nothing to be embarrassed about." Why was he reassuring her? A thread of impatience pulled at him. To know what she was hiding. Why his mother felt the need to bring her. Why she was an advocate for veterans.

"You have family in the service?"

She tensed. At least, he thought she did. But then she sighed and met his gaze. "No, but someone I cared about," she said.

"Past tense," he read into her words. "This person die?"

"Not exactly." She drew in a firming breath and peeled off the wall. "I really don't want to talk about it."

"Understood." But did he? Was she not sharing because she'd tip her hand? Or because it really was painful. He extended a hand. "Ready?"

Ignoring his help, she started climbing again with more strength and confidence. Or was that annoyance. At him?

As he opened the door to the main deck salon, he spotted a steward coming up from the lower deck. "Oi, bring a tonic and some dry bickies?" When the steward nodded, Eamon steered Warren into the salon of the main deck. He started for the rail but realized she'd stopped short just inside the door. "Take the chaise," he said, indicating the lounge a few meters from the rail."

"Won't that make me more sick?"

"Need to look at the horizon, rest, and let your brain reset the signals hitting it."

With a shaky breath, she complied. Stretched herself onto the chaise, crossing her legs at the ankles.

"Head back." He nodded to the moon's reflection rippling on the water. "Look at the horizon." Rather than hover over her, he went to the rails and let the churning wake of the *ViCross*'s engines steady his own nerves, tracing the western coast of the gulf. Maybe the family member hadn't died, but a part of him had in combat? That could be what she meant by "not really." He'd seen it time and again. Soldiers left home the boy their mother had raise and returned shoved into manhood—and brokenness at times—by combat.

"You play nursemaid to seasick guests often?"

"No," he said firmly. "Don't often have guests on my boat."

She chuckled. "I've been on many boats, but this isn't a boat."

"In technical terms it is."

She breathed a laugh. "This has more luxury than a palace—and it's very well done."

Eamon focused on the blue-green waters of the Gulf of Carpentaria. Not on the admiration in her voice. So. Money, power. Was that what she chased? Why she was here? Why did it disappoint him to think that was what she wanted when he'd expected it? And why wasn't he digging through her stories and getting her to talk so she'd betray herself. Betray whatever it as she and his mum were hiding?

"Why the super yacht?" she asked, her voice softer than

before.

Eamon glanced back at her, but found her studying the horizon as instructed. "What do you see?" he asked, returning his attention to the water churning a foamy wake beneath the engines.

"Water," she laughed.

"And?"

"The moon and stars."

"What else?"

Silence gathered between them. "Nothing."

"Exactly," he said, nodding and sliding a smirk in her direction. She studied him with a squint, then slowly pushed her gaze back to the water. A breeze stirred around them, tussling her long red hair. He redirected his gaze. "What even most Aussies don't know about is the Morning Glory."

"The flower?"

"No, the thousand kilometer clouds that ripple across the gulf."

"A thousand kilometers?"

Eamon nodded. "Pilots and gliders love to surf them."

"Would love to see that."

"It's a sight, for sure."

"The water, the clarity . . . " She breathed it in. Smiled. "I get it now."

Her words surprised him. Did she? "Most people can't stand the isolation."

"But you're not alone," she said, drawing her legs to her chest. "You have your crew, the Tri-S team."

"Yeh." Exactly. Why did it alarm him that she understood?

"Sir."

Eamon pivoted and saw the steward waiting with a tray. With thanks, he accepted the glass and biscuits, then set it on the table near the chaise and handed her the glass. "Sip slowly."

"What is it?"

He felt the coolness of her touch, the tremble of her hands. Wondered at the dart that pinched between his shoulders. "Ginger ale." He lowered himself onto a deck chair, staring out at the moonlit waters, debating with himself on how hard to push for answers or just keep his trap shut. It wasn't fair to drill her when she was sick. But then—if she hadn't come on his boat, she wouldn't be sick. "You've known my mum long?"

"A while."

Vague. "She must think a lot of you to bring you, yet she's never mentioned you to me."

"You spend a lot of time with her then?"

Disappointed with himself over the answer he'd have to give, Eamon eyed her, wondering at the question. Was it a jibe? Was she pushing back what he gave?

"Alaina is a person unto herself," she went on, relieving him of the obligation to answer her question, "and I'm just honored to be a part of her world."

That wasn't the answer he'd expected. "You think that highly of her then?"

"I do." She sipped again and leaned back again, her voice strengthening a little.

It did strange things to him hearing someone else speak so fondly, intimately, of his mother. "Why?"

After another sip, she peered past him, eyes narrowing in thought. "She is one of the truest people—women—I've known. She takes over when necessary, but she's also content to let others be in charge." She lifted her shoulders, red coils bunching around her chin as to emphasize the contrast of color. "She has earned the loyalty and admiration of her peers. When she walked in the dining room tonight, the men there were largely changed, their manners, their voices. She commands respect simply by being an honorable, reasonable person."

"Reasonable."

Warren smiled. "You're her son. You're not supposed to find her reasonable."

Her words tugged at the corners of his lips.

"I've learned much from her, and I hope to continue learning."

Why was she learning from his mother? His mum had all but shoved him out the door when he was at home. But then again, he hadn't been the easiest to get along with in the years between losing little Ellis—she had never been Lady Victoria Ellis Rostov-Leclair to him—and entering the military. Thoughts still plagued him of what she could've been, the little firecracker. He'd rather have been on a date but he'd always looked after her when their families were together. But she had a wicked-sharp mind, deviously plotting anything to avoid bedtime. He shook off the sanguine thoughts and asked after her family. "What of your own mother?"

A blander smile colored her expression now as she tilted her head from side to side. "She's busy helping my father run their kingdom."

"Kingdom." Interesting choice of words. Then again, hadn't his father viewed his role in Parliament as the same? Part of the reason Eamon served in the military. He wanted to be a man of action, not of words. "Any siblings?"

"Goodness gracious, Eamon."

He rose at his mother's voice and propriety, irritated that he'd been interrupted. More so that he hadn't seen her come in.

"Hayley isn't feeling well, and rather than seeing to her wellbeing, you're interrogating her."

"Distracting her," he corrected, "with conversation. Giving her mind time to reset and align the horizon with its pull." He nodded to the table. "Fizzy drink and bickies."

Warren shoved to her feet.

Too fast.

Sure enough, she sucked in a breath and covered her

mouth, realizing her mistake. Eamon was rushing her when she swayed hard. He slid an arm around her waist and pulled her against his chest, steadying her. "Easy."

Catching his arm for balance, she darted wide eyes to his. And went still. Her gaze bounced to his and he felt that strange pinch again. Noted she didn't quite reach his shoulder in height. Fit well in his arms, against his side. A buzz—different from the earlier one—started at the back of his brain, traveled down his neck and shoulder and around the arm that held her. The fingers pressed against the curve of her hip.

Her gaze struck his and traced his face, drifted back to his eyes with a wavering smile.

That's when the freckles distracted him again, those sparse dots sprinkled across the bridge of her nose and cheeks. She was very pretty but she was also cute. Couldn't help but think there was a lot of personality hidden beneath that tense surface.

Their surroundings—his mum watching them—clapped into his awareness. "You should sit back down."

"I think you might be right," she whispered.

Eamon eased her to the chaise, then lifted her legs onto the lounger. "Horizon, remember?"

"Right. Horizon," she murmured, darting her gaze from him to the sea.

He straightened, contemplated her for a moment. The wavy red hair, strands whipping across her face. Wide almost fearful eyes. Lips parked in a perpetual smile. Hesitation guarding her movements. He didn't want her to be afraid of him. Where the thought came from, he didn't know. But it was stronger than anything he'd felt in a long time.

Exfil. He needed an exfil.

As if on cue, the thwumping of rotors reached his ears. He checked the sky, grateful for the pale moonlight that revealed the incoming helo with its red blinking safety light. Inwardly he groaned that more guests were en route. But this was also the exfil he needed. He steered his mother toward Warren. "You can tend her now?"

She smiled—a dangerous, knowing one. "I'm quite capable of tending my guest, Eamon."

"Miss Warren." He nodded at the young woman, then his mother. "Mum."

Even as he walked away, he realized he'd failed. He'd gone in to gather information and came out with more questions. She'd worked with his mum. But on what project? She hadn't mentioned that. He needed to find out. And he cursed himself because he could feel it, could feel the inch beneath his barrier under which she'd slipped past.

He slammed it back down and drew his sights on one thing: If he could sort out what project she worked on with his mother, he could then narrow down what felt wrong about Hayley Warren.

CHAPTER 4

"Feeling better?"

Pineapple chunks squeezed between the tongs she held, Ellis glanced over her shoulder where Eamon's security officer stood, wearing a huge grin as he reached for a plate. "I am. Thank you."

"Takes some getting used to, being on a ship like this."

She added more fruit, then continued down the buffet line to the eggs and sausage. "I'm learning that."

"But Titanis took care of you." Tariq reached around her again, snagging a biscuit.

"That's what he does," came the sterner voice of the man who'd sat across from her at dinner last night.

"That's Thorsen," Tariq said. "We call him Thor, though."

Ellis eyed the man and gave him a nod, but didn't appreciate the way he seemed to stare through her. She guessed he was loyal to Eamon, whose uncertainty about her identity and why she was here probably translated to his men.

"Two-way bridge. He looks out for us," Thor said, grabbing a plate and toast at the same time. "And we look out for him."

Just as she expected. She noticed the additional twenty or so guests, all who'd had some role in either Eamon's life or the growth of the veteran's complex. They'd arrived on the chopper that had taken Eamon and his questions away last night. Her gaze snagged on Senator Dietz. He had been the reason their plan had taken so long to come to fruition. She'd have to find a way to talk with him, thank him for joining their initiative and agreeing to come this weekend.

But then her gaze struck a familiar face. It shouldn't have jarred her to see the man who served as her personal security for the last six years. But it had. Because she'd deliberately not wanted him here. Especially with Eamon hawking her every move. She also had to admit, she noticed the way Reggie's protection had turned to attraction in the last year or two. She'd ignored it. Pretended she didn't see it.

"Hey, princess," Reggie Haworth said as he sidled up.

"I'm surprised you're here." Though Ellis tried to keep her tone pleasant, it hitched. "There was no need. I told you—"

"It's my job." He picked a pineapple from her plate and popped it in his mouth.

She scowled at him. "What could happen on a yacht, Reggie?"

"You'd be surprised." Now he stole an apple slice.

Ellis angled her food out of reach. "I'm fine. And get your own food."

"Are you going to eat her entire meal, Reginald Junior?" Alaina's perturbed voice cut into their conversation. She settled her attention on Ellis. "I have some details to work out with you. Do you have a moment?"

"Of course," Ellis said, sure Alaina was simply providing a way to escape Reggie. They excused themselves and made their way to a table beneath the canopy. "Thank you for the rescue."

"When did he become so . . . familiar with you?"

"About a year ago," Ellis said with a groan, stabbing a piece of sausage.

"So you're not comfortable with his attention?"

"No," Ellis said with a laugh. "I've ignored it—and him. But he's watched over me for so long . . . "

"I'll take care of it," Alaina said, lifting a hand, probably to flag down one of the wait staff. "What happened last night before I arrived and stopped Eamon's probing?"

Ellis smiled. "He was quite intent on digging something out of me. Used you—asked how long I'd known you. Why I worked with you. I don't think I gave away anything."

Shaking her perfectly coiffed head, Alaina gave a sad smile. "He was always a clever boy. We'll need to be sure he doesn't corner you again to pry out more." She tore off the corner of her toast and tucked the piece into her mouth. Chewed, while nodding. "He'll figure it out if we aren't careful."

"That's what I'm afraid of. It's probably my fault—coming up on him in the pool. I had no right to be down there, and that set him off."

"Mm, yes. And the way he looked at you—he's trying to figure you out. He knows something's off." Dusting her hands together, she sighed. "Maybe it's good that Reginald Junior is here. He can be distraction enough."

"That may well be true, but I will *not* entertain his advances."

"I would never suggest it," Alaina said, inclining her head to something at the far end of the salon. "Eamon is already onto him."

Ellis glanced in that direction. Her heart rattled in her chest at the sight of Eamon and Reggie engaged in terse conversation. Sleeves partially rolled up, revealing the edge of that tattoo sleeve, Eamon had his hands loose at his sides. Not loose as in relaxed. But loose as in ready to put them to use, to fight.

Reggie scowled at him.

The scene was silly, really. Reggie stood a foot shorter and much less . . . less than Eamon with his six-foot-six height. "That doesn't look good."

"Actually, it does," Alaina said.

"How is that good?"

"If I'm guessing right, Eamon's staking his claim on his turf. And Reggie probably feels the need to do the same since you're here. Having them both fighting over you is perfect. Eamon will be diverted from his mission to rout your secret." Alaina scooped up some food, then lifted a finger. "Reginald said the papers were ready?"

Both fighting over her? She could only be so lucky to have Eamon that attentive. She redirected her thoughts to the question. "He said Mr. Straider will bring them when he arrives on Sunday."

"I'll call Arthur tonight and verify it, just to be sure."

Excitement thrummed through Ellis. "I can't believe it's finally happening." She stole a glance at Eamon. "He's wanted this for so long, but we were defeated many times. It seemed impossible."

"And his advocate, Vic Toriael, succeeded where even Eamon could not," Alaina laughed.

Vic Toriael. It was a derivation of Ellis's full name, Victoria Ellis Rostov-Leclair. The great deception. The one she prayed he wouldn't hold against her.

"I know you've never been comfortable with letting him believe he was dealing with a man instead of you," Alaina said. "but it was imperative. Especially after that Shrew. He never would've given you the time of day."

"I just hope I don't regret letting him believe the mistake." A technology glitch had somehow scrambled part of her name and the message. At least, that's what Alaina had said, but Ellis wondered more than once how a virus ate part of a message but not the rest. When Eamon had written back, saying he wanted to hear more about her venture, that he was interested in investing in the veterans' complex, he'd addressed it to "Mr. Toriael." Ellis had panicked, talked to Alaina, who convinced her to just answer him. Never clarify her name.

That was nearly two years ago, right after the mission that killed his mate. Scarred him. When she'd been so desperate to somehow help him, to be a part of his life again.

"Relax, love," Alaina said, resting her hand over Ellis's. "He's my son, and I will take care of it if necessary."

"Take care of what?" Eamon said, appearing—it seemed—out of thin air with a plate of food. He settled into the seat across from Ellis, nodding a greeting at her. "What is my dear mother interfering with now?"

"Honestly, Eamon. You're going to make me angry with your sneaking about," Alaina complained, then waved her bejeweled hand. "We were discussing your bad manners last night toward Hayley." Alaina taunted him, motioning to Ellis. "You offended her, and therefore me."

"No. I mean . . ." How did her tongue always fail her when he was around? "Eamon was very good to me. Rescued me from humiliating myself more than I already had."

"Mm," Alaina said, but then narrowed her eyes. "Who is that, Eamon?"

Bread in one hand, fork in another, he slid his gaze down the table to the doors where two men entered. "More of your guests," he said with a shrug.

"I don't recognize him." She shrugged. "But then, I haven't personally met everyone I've invited. It wasn't possible."

Eamon frowned. "You have strangers on my boat?"

"On your floating city?"

He took a few bites, then skated his gaze around. "What's Junior doing here?" Eamon asked, putting away his food with ease and speed.

Alaina gave an exaggerated sigh. "His father said he needed a distraction from a bad break-up." She sat back, resting her hands on the arms of the chair. "Sometimes, children need their parents' help."

With a grin that could stop a girl's heart, Eamon said, "Not as much as parents believe, though." He nodded to Ellis. "Do your parents interfere with your life this much?"

"Worse," she said, rolling her eyes. Granted, there'd been a very good reason for that. One that still made her a little more than nervous to be without protection, which was why they'd asked Reggie to keep an eye out for her when they went to uni together. "But I suppose they mean it for the best."

"See?" His mother laughed "Even she can see the benefit."

"But she"—he stabbed those blue eyes at her—"wants to impress you because she admires you, so of course she'll side with you."

"Side with her?" Ellis nearly choked.

His expression went flat, serious. "Then you don't agree with her?"

Ellis groan-laughed. "Don't you dare tangle me up in that."

He grinned. "Smart girl."

Girl? *Girl?!?* She was twenty-five! He might have nine years on her, but she was hardly that young. In fact, she was convinced she was too old to still be single. But that was another matter altogether.

"You've worked with my mother for two years now, yes?"

"One." Her heart tripped over his obvious ploy to trip her up with bad information. "Right." He cut into a steak. "So, do I know your parents?"

Alaina slapped his arm. "I warned you about this last night. No more, Eamon. No more!" She huffed and scooted back. "Now, this very smart girl and I need to do some work. You will be up for the lunch, won't you?"

It wasn't a question and apparently Eamon noticed as well. "I do have a company to run. You realize that, right?"

His mother stood and Eamon came to his feet. "So you'll be there?"

He kissed her cheek, the only sign of acquiescence he gave. Ellis managed a smile, appreciating the relationship between mother and son. Eamon again acknowledged her with a nod, his expression stiff. Not severe, but also not far from it. She felt his eyes on her as she followed Alaina.

"Mrs. Straider," a man said, stepping into her path.

"Ah, Mr. Lynwood. So glad you could come."

His eyes gleamed. "I wouldn't miss this!"

"Have you met Miss Warren?"

His eyebrows rose. "Miss Warren—it is truly an honor. What you've accomplished is nothing short of a miracle."

Ellis smiled. "Thank you, sir. It has been a long, hard road, but I'm very glad to have it sorted now."

"Indeed!"

Ellis felt the pull to glance back at Eamon—a mistake. Her gaze collided with his. And he wasn't the type to look away, to pretend he wasn't staring. Not because he found her attractive. But because he found her suspicious.

"If you will excuse us, Mr. Lynwood," Alaina said as she took a step away. "Miss Warren and I would love to talk to you more—we are so grateful for your very generous contributions—"

"It's my honor. I believe in this!"

"Brilliant. Just remember—mum's the word for now." Alaina touched a manicured hand to her lips. "If you will excuse us for the moment. Miss Warren and I have some work to tend to. Let's talk more this evening."

"Of course."

Ellis opened the glass door and held it for Alaina. They left the upper deck and headed to the main deck where their suites were. Rounding the stairs, Ellis finally took a steadying breath. She'd been so afraid Eamon would hear or follow.

"I still can't believe you got that man to part with his money," Alaina said with a laugh as she let them into her suite. She crossed the thickly padded carpet to the sitting area.

The luxury of the yacht still amazed Ellis, especially the staterooms with their fine appointments, which were as big, if not bigger than her own bedroom in her flat.

"Believe me. It wasn't easy. There's a reason he's a

millionaire—he hoards his money." She laughed and shook her head, reclining on the settee.

"Not true of all rich men. Look at my Eamon," Alaina corrected. "He'd give it all away—and is going to part with a ridiculous chunk—to insure wounded veterans have a home."

"And hope." Ellis thought back to the most recent email he'd sent to "Vic," encouraging "him" to be more assertive and insist that the benefactors and politicians come together to make this happen. The plan, he said, had stagnated too long. Lives were slipping through their hands. *The U.S. loses twenty veterans—Oz not as much but far too much—every single day. It's unacceptable and an egregious failure of society. It has to stop but it won't until we do something.*

"A part of me hates to see you so besotted, Ellis," Alaina said.

She wanted to argue. To tell Alaina she was drawn to Eamon's character, his heart—which she was. But Poseidon had nothing on the man who'd erupted out of that pool. It was like the frosting on a tiramisu cupcake. Even if she didn't argue, what could she say?

"He has vowed to never marry. And despite his very intense interest in you, which I know goes beyond his instincts picking up nuances as well as the sliver of cracks in your contrived identity and purpose, he is a very stubborn man. Even beyond that, he would have to find out who you really are, and that"—she shook her head gravely—"that is a very dangerous road." She pointed that manicured hand. "That he might find unforgiveable."

True. Terribly true. And Ellis had resolved herself to that early in their communication trail that led to this weekend. "I don't expect anything of him, except that he will work with me to make the complex happen, because that is his dream as much as mine. Though he may hate me later, he will want to see it built and come to life." She forced herself to accept that might be the extent of their future. "If only that, I will be happy."

"Will you?"

"I choose to be."

Alaina drew in a long breath and slowly released it, then poured herself some water and joined Ellis at the table. "We should go over the presentation ceremony. Handling this correctly is crucial to Eamon's response."

"It'd be nice," Ellis said, "if we could go to the upper deck and walk through things, too."

"Tricky that—very close to Eamon's command and owner's deck. If he saw us . . ." She sipped her water. "Maybe once everyone has gone to bed we can give it a try." She scooted closer, looking at the laptop. "Show it to me again."

With pleasure, Ellis pulled out the architect's rendering of the conversion of the abandoned hotel into a multi-storied complex that would house veterans, provide grocery stores, clothes stores, a small college campus, medical facilities, and so much more. It'd been Eamon's brainchild. And he'd chosen Vic Toriael—Ellis, unwittingly—as his partner to build the venture and bring it to fruition. It was, in essence, their dream.

WHY WOULDN'T SHE answer questions about her parents? He hadn't asked anything complicated. Sitting at his desk in his private quarters, Eamon cuffed a hand over his mouth and stared at her picture on his screen. What was she hiding? Why else would she avoid questions? And him?

Okay, so he complicated things by probing. Nobody liked when others dug into their business. He got that. But he'd never been one to ignore the buzzing at the back of his head. It'd never steered him wrong.

Until Brie.

No, that hadn't been the buzzing. That was idiocy.

He shifted in his seat. That wasn't the problem here. His interest in Hayley Warren went beyond attraction. He wanted to get into the truth.

But his mum.

What was with that? Why was his mum complicit in whatever Warren was up to? Didn't add up. She'd always been his advocate. She wouldn't put him in danger or do anything to hurt him, but she wasn't above pushing a woman on him that she thought could be a good match. Granted, she hadn't done it since before Brie, but what other reason could there be for this circus?

Staring at her likeness, Eamon leaned back in his seat, the chair creaking in protest. *What are you up to?* Her eyes. There was something familiar about her eyes. He magnified the image and saw flecks of green and brown there. Did she realize the smattering of freckles on her right cheek almost resembled the Southern Cross?

Eamon dropped back. *Right. You've been staring too long at this picture.* He shoved out of his seat and accessed the Command hub to find Tariq. Drill him on what he'd found so far. Stepping through the hatch, he heard his steps echo through the hub. Computers thrummed and the normal boat noises came, but no voices. Empty.

What . . .? Where were they? He glanced at the wall clock. 2130 hours. No wonder the place sat deserted. He moved into the concourse of the upper deck. Music, voices, and laughter drew him down to the main deck where he spotted Tariq and Thor chatting with a crew of seven. His mother wasn't here, which was unusual. She normally stayed late, entertaining her guests. She wasn't the average sixty-something mother, who retired early for her beauty rest. He reached for the door when a noise snagged his attention.

Turning his head, he listened. Closed out the main deck salon. Homed in . . . More voices. Terse. Below. He descended to the lower deck, quieting his approach. If this was a couple quarrel, it was none of his business. When his foot hit the marble floor, he heard *thwats*. His heart jarred, thinking silenced weapons. But no. No, that was more like hands swatting clothing.

He followed it to the VIP suites. Bounced a look around the corner. His two-second recon irritated him. *Just move on. It's none of your business.* He edged out a little, exposing his position to Warren, who stood with Reggie Junior, twenty paces from him.

The sight went sideways through Eamon. Lover's quarrel?

But then Reggie gripped her arm and yanked her closer.

"Stop it," Hayley hissed, wrenching free. She tried to wedge past him, but Junior wasn't having it.

No lesser man than the one who preyed on women. "There a problem here?" he heard himself ask.

The two jerked toward him.

"Nah," Junior said, lifting his chin. "You can go back upstairs."

Eamon advanced a step. Squared his shoulders and lifted his chin. Who did this dimwit think he was telling Eamon where he could go on his own boat?

"Eamon," Warren said, anchoring onto him. "Could I talk to you?" Her eyes—hidden from Junior—went wide, pleading as she drew closer.

Head ringing at the way she sought safety with him, Eamon nodded and reached for her, touching her arm as she slid past him. When Reggie started after her, Eamon angled to block the narrow gangway. Reggie locked onto Warren and kept coming. Would the guy actually try him?

Eamon snapped his palm out and with the momentum Reggie had, it struck his chest, sending him back a couple of steps. When the man's surprised gaze flung to Eamon's, he said, "Private conversation." Even though he felt her absence, Eamon remained a barricade.

"Hayley, c'mon," Reggie said with a nervous laugh. "You

know I'm just looking out for you."

Ignoring the strange dart of jealousy that hit his chest, Eamon snorted and turned to Warren, who was already on the stairs. He glanced back to find a red-faced Junior. "Nick off."

Hands fisted, Junior clearly wanted to try something. But he knew better.

A shame. It'd be nice to teach him a lesson. Eamon had itched to flog him since their childhood when Junior's cowardice endangered Eamon's life and got a girl killed.

"You don't even know," Junior hissed.

"You're whinging." He shot him a warning look, then leaned in, lowering his voice. "Don't treat her like that again."

"Or what?"

He nearly smiled. "Try me." Letting his warning hang, Eamon pivoted and took the stairs, slow enough to be sure Junior didn't reach Warren. When he gained the main deck and peered through the glass doors, he searched for her in the crowded salon.

"Thank you." Her quiet voice yanked him to where she stood beneath a dome light in the passage. Light haloed her reddish-blonde hair. He couldn't help searching out the Southern Cross on her cheek, but as he did, Eamon realized she was close. Not even a proper distance from him as she graced him with a sheepish grin. "Truthfully, I didn't want to talk to you. Just needed an escape path."

He nodded, catching a whiff of some floral scent. Shampoo? Perfume? *You were looking into her past, remember?* "What did he want with you?"

"What he's wanted for the last year."

So she knew Junior was interested in her. Was the interest mutual? "Did I interfere?"

"What?" She gaped. "No!" She deflated. "I suppose it's my own fault for not telling him flat-out to leave me alone, but he's . . . a longtime friend. He's watched out for me. I guess in a way, I feel like I owe him. What he did down there isn't really like Junior. Guess he misjudged." She shook her head. "He's . . . misguided."

"No, he's Junior," Eamon said.

"There is that." Her smile was genuine.

And he felt it. Felt the warmth of it in his gut. Noticed how the photo on his monitor didn't do justice to her eyes. He tilted his head again to see her Southern Cross freckles, realizing only when her gaze started bouncing from his chest to his face that he'd somehow moved closer.

"You going in there?" she asked, nodding toward the salon.

He skidded a gaze to where an animated Tariq was sharing something with the crowd. That'd been him once. A long time ago. "Nah. Long day tomorrow."

"Well." She shrugged. "I think I'll stay a while before heading back down and risking Junior again."

"Sounds smart," he said.

"Well, g'night. And thanks." She slipped through the door and strode to the middle of the salon.

He told himself he stood in the gangway watching her integrate with the crowd to insure her safety, to confirm Junior didn't reattempt to manhandle her. He'd done that once before—looked for reasons to be near Brie.

Annoyed with himself, Eamon started away. Five paces later, a burst of laugher rolled out from the salon. From Warren. It stilled him. Pulled him back. Staying in the shadows of the gangway, he watched as Tariq included her in his animated story. She was laughing. They all were.

What was the story?

Eamon slipped inside and tucked himself in the corner, listening. But even as he did, the crowd broke up and drifted to the far deck to play shuffleboard. Music filtered in, luring some into dancing. Warren stayed close to Thor and Tariq. More interesting was that she fell into a discussion—not intense but not far from it—with the senators and Haworth.

The men clustered around her, the conversation focused but casual.

They know her.

How would they know her if he didn't? Hadn't even heard of her until she showed up on the guest list. Eamon rubbed his jaw, watching as she dusted her red hair from her shoulder and sipped a fizzy drink.

Go to bed. Trouble starts with curiosity.

As do fact-finding missions.

"Hayley," Tariq called loudly.

Eamon monitored as she glanced over her shoulder with a curious smile.

"I challenge you to a game of shuffleboard."

She laughed, but then excused herself from the stuffy-shirts, set aside her drink, and accepted the paddle from Tariq. "I'm not very good at this," she warned.

Maybe she'd let slip some truth while playing shuffleboard that would peel back the layers of this deceptively sweet onion. He should stick around. But then—then Tariq slid an arm around her as he explained how to get a better score. The arm wasn't necessary.

Eamon tensed, irritated. Tariq knew better than to come on to a guest. Tariq's gaze hit Eamon's. And he straightened. Shifted away.

Better.

Warren looked in his direction and hesitated. Stared. Eamon riveted his feet to his spot, forbidding himself to follow the impulse to cross the deck and join them.

"Hey," Thorsen said, sidling over to Warren, catching her hand, and leading her to the dance floor.

Even as she turned into Thor's hold, Warren slid another green-eyed glance in his direction. There was a message in that, but it was one he told himself not to read into. But the warning came too late. Did she want him to join them? The glance wasn't shy. It was direct. Curious.

Thor said something to her, distracting Warren from Eamon. Then she laughed. So did Thor.

Eamon clenched his teeth. *Why haven't you left yet?*

Didn't Tariq and Thor have work to do? Backgrounds to probe? Security to secure?

Stepping and twirling, Warren proved she had dance skills. But he didn't like how close Thor held her. The way he drew her closer, swirled her around a little rougher than necessary, forcing her to fall against his chest.

That's your imagination, mate. Thor was married with an ankle biter.

"A drink, sir?"

Eamon flinched at the voice to his left. The bartender. He glanced back to the corner he'd started in. Then back to Thor dancing with Warren.

With a flourish, Tariq struck the puck. It went wild. Gained air. Sailed toward the dance floor.

Eamon surged to intercept the disaster.

But Thor spun Warren out.

She whirled.

The puck clattered over the deck, decidedly sliding toward her. Right under her feet.

Eyes wide, Warren stumbled with a yelp. Stepped back, laughing. But the next step—landed her on the puck again. Her foot whooshed backward.

Warren pitched forward. Though Thor tried to catch her, she fumbled right into Eamon. How he'd gotten close enough to catch her, he didn't know, but was surprised when she flopped against him.

His arms were around her before he could register it. She clamped small hands around his forearms. Eyes wide, hair dangling across her brow, Warren froze, lips parted in a silent 'oh' as she slowly staggered upright. He steadied her. The blush from the dancing and merriment deepened into something more.

He pushed the tangle of red from her face, startling himself. And her. She drew in a quiet breath as those green eyes flecked with caramel locked onto him. Her laughter trickled away. Her smile faded. Stopped.

"Sorry," she whispered, pulling free.

Something in him recoiled. Tightened. That she pulled back. That she lost her smile. That he scared her.

Mostly that.

He released her. Noted the way the others were watching, quiet but attentive. Watching with sidelong glances. Hayley shifted back another step. "Do—"

Eamon strode from the salon, shedding the fire roiling in his lungs. The anger speeding through his veins over the way she reacted—*negatively*—to him. It angered him that he was ropeable. He didn't care. She was trouble. Questions loomed around her like a dead weight.

This was not happening. He would *not* go down again.

Never again.

And that meant it was time to do everything he could to get to the bottom of whatever lie Hayley Warren perpetuated.

CHAPTER 5

SINK OR SWIM.
 Oh. Bad choice of metaphors.

Ellis surveyed the main salon deck, tables and lounge chairs cleared away in the night. Tables were elaborately decorated with blue hydrangeas to accent the gray and blue décor of the salon. Candelabras gleamed and tables waited elegantly for their guests. In the middle, a dais sported a table and lectern, where she would announce the miraculous success of the project. The one she worked on with Eamon. But not with Eamon. Around him. That wasn't exactly right either. Worked deceptively with Eamon.

She groaned and shoved her hair back from her face, trying desperately not to remember the tight embrace of last night.

Okay. Not an embrace. He'd caught her, intervening her clumsy slip on the puck. But those arms had tightened around her like steel bars. Steadied her. Warming her from the inside out. She'd straightened, feeling like she'd been secured to him with industrial glue. Then it'd been the way he'd looked at her. The searching—scary because she wasn't sure if it'd been his mission to find out what she was hiding, but then he'd swept the hair from her face.

She touched her cheek, still feeling the heat of his touch. That's when she'd known it wasn't the mission that had him staring at her.

At least, she hoped it wasn't. But then he'd stalked out.

Not angrily but definitely *done* with them, with her.

"You've done an amazing job, my dear," came Alaina's soft voice. "It's stunning! But I'm going to guess that wistful look on your face isn't about the table settings."

Ellis smiled guiltily. They'd resolved that she should stay away from him, but he was like this super-magnet. Every time she turned around, he was there. And she wanted him there.

"What happened?"

"It was silly really," she said, anxious for the story to be told. "I was dancing—"

"With Eamon?"

"With Mr. Thorsen. But then the shuffleboard puck skidded across the deck. Tripped me. I nearly twisted my ankle and . . ." Telling his mum she fell into his arms would make her sound desperate and feel embarrassed. "Eamon caught me."

"He was here? In the salon, socializing?" Incredulity piqued her voice.

This time Ellis laughed. "I'm not sure I'd call it *socializing*. He mostly stayed in the shadows."

"So you couldn't see him watching you."

Was that a question? Ellis searched Alaina's face for mockery. But there was none. In fact, there seemed to be a lot of concern. Maybe even more of that fear. "I should've known you'd catch his eye. But he'll turn that against you—and himself."

"How do you mean?"

"He'll dig harder and deeper than ever before, determined to prove you aren't who you say you are."

"But I'm *not* who I say I am," Ellis breathed, her pulse racing.

"You are, darling. You are every bit the person making this announcement, who's worked so hard to make it happen. A name is but a label easily changed."

"I doubt Eamon will see it that way."

"We have to make him see it that way." She turned to Ellis. "Change of plans."

Feeling the need for support, Ellis wrapped her arms around herself and nodded.

"During this afternoon's socializing, I want you to seek him out."

"What!?"

"Seek him out. Ask him to dance."

"But that . . ." In his arms. Against that incredibly sculpted chest and crushed between those biceps? Stare into those blue eyes? "I couldn't. He would—"

"Right now, you're prey because you're skulking away from him. It's set off his warning bells. So, you're going to turn it around on him. Turn into him. Draw him in. Distract him with your intelligence and beauty."

"That sounds sexist."

"Honey, if it works, then do it. We don't need Eamon deciding he has to shut down the event because he's figuring things out about you."

She widened her eyes. "He'd do that?"

"In a split-second if he has any proof."

Ellis scanned the tables, florals. "But all the money for the event—"

Alaina scoffed. "Haven't you learned yet that Eamon Straider would risk his entire fortune to protect himself?" She started for the door. "That scar on his face? It went straight into his heart."

HIS GRANDFATHER TOLD him once that the best way to make God laugh was to tell Him your plans. And it definitely seemed like God was laughing at him tonight. Though he'd focused on the crowd mingling, some talking, some dancing,

Eamon somehow had an invisible radar with Hayley Warren's name on it.

On the arm of Haworth, she entered wearing a dress that reminded him of the night sky the way the navy fabric glittered as she moved. The left shoulder was enticingly bare and the right had a sheer fabric that rippled down her arm. The fabric clung to curves intended to distract and disorient. Though she wasn't wearing a formal dress, she'd gone all out. Wasn't it overkill?

Dressed to kill.

Or distract. Thirty guests and his mind targeted her—had she done it intentionally? Teeth set on edge, he snatched a drink from the steward's tray. Just ignore her. Stay safe. Something was off.

Yeah, my equilibrium.

Brie had grabbed his attention. But this girl... she grabbed his whole mind. He tossed back the drink and set it down on a table. When he pivoted, he stilled, air trapping in his throat.

"Hello, Mr. Straider."

Thoughts trapped in the vortex of her sweet voice and light perfume, he nodded as she glided up beside him. "Miss Warren." That dress made her complexion look fairer, softer. He'd never forget the touch of her skin against his fingertips last night. But now he wanted a refresher course.

Guests. Look at the guests.

"You look quite dapper in a tux," she said.

Was her voice shaking or was it his imagination? "You kidding? This penguin suit doesn't make anyone look dapper." Better stick close to the target. Get them comfortable. Get them talking. Wait for her to slip up, right? But he didn't trust himself, or her. "If you'll—"

"Care to dance?"

He stilled. Glanced at her, but she was watching the crowd. She swallowed. What was she up to?

She's nervous. Because of me.

This could be her trying to outfox him. Play his game. The thought amused him. "Sure."

A wavering smile fell across her lips as he extended his hand. Her fingers were warm, but clammy. He nearly smirked. They turned into each other and came together naturally, gracefully. He slipped a hand to the small of her back, but did his best to keep his touch light. She said nothing as they danced, and he was glad. It was hard enough to think with her in his arms, her curves pressed again him. Besides, he wasn't up to conversation this early in the day, not when he'd have to entertain into the evening.

"I haven't seen your mum," Warren noted as they glided around the deck.

"In the corner with Reginald," he said, nodding in that direction.

Her expression brightened. "Ah. She looks lovely." Warren's left hand rested on his upper arm.

"So, you work with her?" His gaze hit his mum, and he couldn't help but notice she seemed ambivalent that he was dancing with Warren. She had been all commando with him, protective and turning him away. "Regularly?"

"Mm," Warren murmured.

"Since my mum is mostly involved in charities, is that a favorite of yours as well?"

"Interrogating me again, Mr. Straider?"

Eamon peered down at her to see her eyes, gauge what emotion sat behind that question. But her gaze was not on him. "You invited me to dance. Are we to do it in silence and tension?"

"Tension?" Her eyes finally came to his.

Wide. Expressive. Sparkling. A very well put-together combination there—with the Southern Cross freckle smattering, the coral-tinged full lips, pert nose, and that ripple of soft red hair that framed her face. "You're uptight," he noted, pressing his hand against the arc of her back that flared from her spine. Lifted the hand he held. "Or do you always dance like this?"

"I rarely dance," she said quickly.

And there he had it. "So, you asked me, why?"

Her gaze darted to his. Color mottled her cheeks. "If you did not want to dance . . . " She loosened her grip and he felt her pull away.

Eamon urged her back into his hold. "Easy, Warren. I'm not that scary, am I?"

"Quite," she said, her with a breath. "I wanted to dance with you because I find you intelligent and handsome—there. Are you pleased?"

He smirked. Did she mean that? Or was she trying to put him on edge?

"And I find your advocacy for veterans quite attra— amazing."

His mind tripped over that last flub of words, but more, it stalled out on something much more noticeable. "How do you know about that?" Nobody knew. He'd kept his donations private.

"Must you ask?" she whispered, the words somehow skidding across the base of his throat.

"I must."

With a huff, she shook her head and rolled her eyes. Released his hand—though when he tried to stop her, she snapped it free. Stopped in her tracks. "Your mother told me." Hurt spiraled through those eyes that reminded him of the Cape on a beautiful day. "Truly, Eamon, if you are to shed the Beast of Cape York moniker, your manners could use some attention." With that, she dove into the crowds. Away from him.

Junior reached out to her, but she lifted a dismissive hand to him, then glanced back at Eamon and shook her head again, disappearing to the port side. Were those tears on her cheeks?

"Eamon, a dance?"

Rubbing his jaw, he wondered at what'd just happened. That he hurt her enough to cause her to cry. Though he was not even sure there were tears. That she had so adamantly refused him the full dance.

"Eamon?"

It took a second for his brain to register the dark-haired woman before him. And her invitation to dance. "No." He took a step away, then remembered the remonstration regarding his manners. "Thank you. I mean—sorry."

Though he wasn't sure what he should do, he found himself going after Warren. Which was a bad idea. Not only was he bad at small talk, but needling still pricked him with suspicion. Something was off. She couldn't have found out about the veterans' donations from his mum because he simply didn't talk about those things with her. Or his father. It wasn't any of their business.

So how had Warren known? He searched the salon deck, but could not find her. Maybe it was just as well. He spotted Tariq near the sundeck rail talking to a man—another Eamon didn't know. There would be a lot of them when the next chopper arrived, also bringing his father to the *ViCross*.

Maybe he just needed some space before it got too crowded.

He thought of going below, but then remembered his first encounter with Warren. When he'd been swimming and working. So, not below deck. He should check in with Captain Ezra. Eamon strode from the salon and pushed through the glass doors. He banked left and headed up the steps to the wheel deck.

Captain Ezra came to his feet when he saw Eamon. "Sir. Everything okay?"

Eamon nodded. "Came to ask you the same thing." He glanced around, knowing he had no need to check things here, but he'd always done so out of respect for the man ferrying him around the waters.

"All's well," Ezra said, raking a hand through his graying wavy hair. "We had one stray, but she's there. Said she just needed some air."

Out the aft windows, he was surprised to find Warren standing alone. Why was he surprised? So far, she had been everywhere she shouldn't be. His irritation must've crossed his face, because Ezra shifted.

"No worries. I told her to stay out there. She'll come in soon enough anyway."

"Yeh?" Eamon squinted, noting—but trying not to—the way the sun caught the glimmering threads of her dress. "Why's that?"

"Next chopper's due within the hour." He nodded to the comms panel.

"Right," he muttered and started for the door. Annoyed she was up here. Relieved she was up here.

Why are you relieved?

Eamon pushed open the door and stepped out into the sunlight. Warren had moved to the round leather seating arrangement in the middle of the sundeck. She was bent forward and, fingers pressed together, she cupped them over her mouth and nose. Eyes closed. Wind whipped her hair in her face and tugged it loose from the bun, but she didn't seem to care or notice.

Now her remonstration sharpened and pierced his pride. Eamon moved to her side and sat down. "You're spot on."

Warren yelped and jerked straight.

"I'm sorry—"

"No." She closed her eyes again and shook her head for the millionth time. "No. It's okay. I was just—I needed some time to—" She was on her feet. "I was just leaving."

Eamon stood. Extended an arm, catching her. "Please. Stay."

"I can't do this, Eamon." That was better than Mr. Straider. "I can't be the bad guy in your book."

"Then in someone else's book?" He'd meant it as a joke.

Warren lifted her palms and stepped back. Her chin dimpled and those full lips flattened. "I can't do this . . ."

"I'm sorry. I—it was poor taste in a joke."

"Joke." Her eyebrow arced and somehow it freed a tear. It slipped down her cheek.

That did something very strange in his chest. Punched the breath from him. As she angled away, Eamon caught her shoulders, staying her departure. He inched closer. "I'm sorry. You . . . there are questions."

She deflated. "I give up, Eamon. I give up. I can't do this. I can't be here to . . ." She seemed to choke on her words. "I can't be here to help Alaina with this evening and have you thinking I'm this person with malicious intent when all I've wanted is your approval."

"Approval?"

Warren dropped her chin, wagging her head back and forth. Then despite the roar of the engines and the thrum of the ship, he felt the slightest bounce to her shoulders. "I told her I couldn't do this—"

"Hey." He hooked a finger under her chin and lifted her gaze to his. Tears made him swim in the depths of her irises. He dragged his knuckles against her cheek to swipe them away. But her eyes hung heavy with hurt and rejection. Grief. The tears came faster, cries turning to sobs. Eamon swept them, wishing he could dam this waterfall. Wishing he hadn't caused it. "Hayley. I'm sorry."

She lifted a hand to wave him off as she had Junior, but her fingertips raked up his stomach, startling them both. She stared at the spot she'd touched. Then touched the buttons. His abdomen.

Eamon slid his hand along her cheek. Thumbed away the last of the tears, fighting the torrent that awakened at her touch. At the way she stilled. Like a rip current, life raging around them, she was there right in the middle of it all. Still. Calm. Drawing him out of his self-imposed isolation. Dragging him from his own warnings to step off.

But he eased in.

Her gaze slowly lifted, as if answering the roar within him.

Eamon homed in on her mouth.

Don't. There are unanswered questions.

Her lips parted, and somehow against the din of the water and the boat, he heard that quick intake of breath. The anticipation of a kiss tightened her hold on him. Like an anchor dragging bottom, life slowed. His heart slowed.

Her breath darted against his lips. Warm. Inviting. He had but to close the millimeters that hung between them vacant.

A shadow spirited over them.

Eamon ducked instinctively, glancing up and seeing the chopper descending to the helo pad on the other side of the wheel deck. Swallowing hard, swiping a hand over his mouth, he turned to Warren, but she was scurrying across the deck and descending into the boat. Taking his idiocy with him.

And anger. Anger that he'd wanted that kiss. Anger that he'd done it again. Fallen for a pair of pretty eyes and lost his brain in the process.

CHAPTER 6

SWIMMING HADN'T HELPED, so Eamon turned to the weights in his stateroom, not daring to set himself up for another encounter with Warren. But here, alone, his thoughts kept wandering to the sundeck. To her soft skin and the line he'd nearly crossed.

Warring with that heated moment, he also struggled to align the facts. She knew things she shouldn't know. Was friends with men she shouldn't be friends with. And his mother...

"Should I know her name?"

Eamon gritted his teeth. "I'm thirty-four, Dad. Surprise inspections expired nearly fifteen years ago." He came to his feet, intentionally exerting his four-inch advantage over his father, who wore a sharp navy suit and had his hair meticulously combed. As always. Eamon extended a hand, drawing him into a one-shouldered hug. "Good to see yeh."

"And you—but I still want to know who my son was kissing on the sundeck."

"I didn't kiss her. It was . . . a misunderstanding. She was upset over"—no need to admit to his own guilt in that—"something and I was trying to reassure her."

His father laughed. "Some reassurance. Let's hope you don't do that to every guest who gets upset."

"I was surprised you agreed to come to one of Mum's events here," Eamon said, pulling a towel from the shelf and hooking it over the shower door.

"And miss seeing my son?"

Eamon eyed him. He had never cared about that before.

His father laughed again. "Barton's here, yeh?"

Eamon nodded.

"That's why."

"The jobs from Japan?" Shower ready, he folded his arms and squared his stance.

His father's expression blanked then brightened. "Right." He clapped Eamon's shoulder. "I'll let you get showered up and see you downstairs for the gala."

With a final nod, Eamon waited until he heard the door click shut. What was that about? Barton was here. But why . . . did his father seem confused?

Too many questions. Not near enough answers.

After a shower and change, Eamon dressed and hurried to the Command deck, taking his tux jacket with him. "Tariq."

Tariq looked up from behind the security hub. "Wasup?"

"What have you found on her?" Quiet amplified each step—insanely quiet against the roar of his pulse and the helo seconds earlier—to his desk, forcing him to check his friend, who had stopped moving.

"Seriously?" Tariq's eyes raged. "After the way she fell into your arms and you nearly kissed her—"

Eamon flung a glare at the guy.

Tariq tapped the monitor. Security feeds. "I am the security chief, after all." He grunted. "And maybe you missed it, but that woman is into you."

"We have thirty people coming on board tomorrow and a girl who doesn't add up."

"She adds up very well, if you ask me. And you know it, too."

Eamon dropped his attention to the file. He fingered apart the pages. Staring at that pretty face. "She's hiding something."

"Besides being terrified of the Beast of Cape York?"

Hands on his belt, Eamon worked to get hold of his anger. Tensed when Thor stepped into the Command deck but said nothing. "Are you telling me you don't have anything?"

Tariq folded his arms. "Titanis, I've gone over her backstory ten times. Her creds are legit. Whatever she's hiding . . ." He shrugged.

"We still haven't found it. My mother's in on it, too," Eamon said, making his point. "I want it found."

Tariq growled. "You have got—"

"She's beautiful, smart," Thor cut in. "Everyone likes her—including you. And that scares you."

Eamon leaned forward, palming his desk, glowering at his security chief through a knotted brow. "What scares me is my ship, my crew, and my guests at risk."

"What risk?" Tariq's voice pitched. "She has no bomb. No guns."

"What're you thinking, Titanis?" Thor said, his tone more of challenge than question. "What threat? What's her motive?"

Eamon swallowed. Scratched his jaw, feeling the twinge of weirdness at the scar that bisected his jaw.

"Besides threatening your self-imposed isolation?" Tariq stomped to Eamon's station. "It's all there. Pristine. Perfect order." He swiped a hand over the papers. "Everything . . ." His gaze skidded back and forth. "Everything in order. Birth and family history. Education . . ." He slowed. His gaze landing on one section. Then another.

Eamon's heart tripped. "What?"

Tariq frowned. "I . . ." Slid around the desk and angled closer. He looked to his computer. Then to the papers.

"Tariq?"

The guy went to his station. Logged in and started hammering on the keyboard.

Thor exchanged a look with Eamon, who suddenly felt a knot of dread twisting his gut. Only then did he realize how badly he *hadn't* wanted there to be anything wrong or off with Warren. Both he and Thor joined Tariq.

Eamon studied the dark features, trying to read what trouble had been spotted. "What'd you see, Tariq?"

The guy looked ready to cry, his disappointment as palpable as Eamon's. "It's all there." His voice was smaller, less strident. "All of it. Perfect. Pristine."

"Yeh. You said that."

Thor shrugged. "So?"

"It's perfect." Nearly black eyes came to his. "*Too* perfect."

Eamon loosened his arms and let them hang at his sides. "Meaning?"

A hissed curse hit the air. "It's fake." Tariq flipped his hand at the monitor. Smacked it. "Her backstory is fake."

"You're sure?" Thor asked the question Eamon couldn't bring himself to voice.

Anger was one thing, but this . . . what does it mean? What was her intent?

"How do you know?" Thor asked.

"Easiest example? It says she was honors." A few clicks and two screens came up, Tariq flicking fingers at them. "Yet she's not on the Honor List. She listed her address and that she lived there for the last ten years."

"Yeh? So?"

"It was demolished six months ago."

"So her resume isn't updated."

"Date is current." Tariq deflated. "Why would she lie about all this?"

"What I want to know," Eamon said, stalking to the door, "is why my mother lied." When he reached the hatch, the proximity sensor went off. He hesitated and glanced back.

Tariq glanced at the security camera and console. "Something big. A biologic, I think." He adjusted some knobs and scanned the feed. "Yeah. Nothing there now. Probably a biologic."

Eamon pushed through the hatch and leapt down the steps to the main deck, scanned the thickening crowd in the salon, but didn't find her. So he slid down below to the VIP staterooms. He gave several hard raps against her door. When she didn't immediately answer, he rapped again. "Mum. We need to talk." Hands on hips, he told himself to stay calm. She had a reason. *Better be a bloody good one.*

"She's not in there."

Eamon pivoted and found Warren holding open her own door. Hair curled around her shoulder and arms hugged her tightly, she did this smile-shrug thing.

"She went for a swim. Said she couldn't sleep."

"A guilty conscience does that to a person."

Warren's face blurred with confusion. She swallowed. "Can I help you with something?"

"No. Thank you." He started for the stairs. Then swung back. "Actually."

Warren shifted. Seemed to tighten her stance.

"Want to tell me why the two of you have been lying to me?"

CHAPTER 7

He would never give up the chase or the scowl. She couldn't tell him all of her secrets, but she could hand him the biggest one that would ruin any hope of holding his respect or getting that kiss he'd withheld on the sundeck. She nodded into her stateroom.

He came to the doorway but no further.

Ellis went to the small desk tucked against the wall and fingered the file. It would not only ruin his perception of her, but weeks of hard work in their attempt to celebrate his dream. The drawings. The contracts. With a sigh of surrender, she lifted it and turned. Bumping right into him. Somehow, he'd silently closed the six-foot gap.

Warmth shot through, remembering how his abs had jounced at her touch on the deck, then the warmth of him through his shirt. The steady advance as he bent to kiss her. But then he hadn't. And it'd been for the best, she supposed now.

His brows tightened. "What is that?" he growled.

She nudged it at him. "You know what it is."

He stared at it. "The complex."

It had to be her imagination that his voice quieted a fraction. "It was supposed to be a surprise." Her heart broke that they couldn't do this in a grand celebration.

He was so close, making the space feel small and... consumed by him. His scent was clean, crisp. Not exactly cologne. Maybe aftershave. "I don't understand."

She lifted her chin. "The funding came through."

"I know that. My advocate—"

"What your *advocate* didn't tell you was that the Honorable Mr. Haworth finally convinced the Honorable Mr. Reighton to approve the proposal."

He flinched. His dark brows knotted. "How do you know so much about this? My mum again?"

"Saying yes would be an easy answer but not exactly the truth." Ellis swallowed. Now or never. Now or never. "I know because . . . *I'm* your advocate."

"Mr. Toriael—"

"It was a mistake," she said meekly. "An email got mangled or something. I'm not really sure." She touched her forehead. "When you responded with interest in the complex but believed you were writing to a man, I'd told your mum and she . . . she felt it best not . . . not to enlighten you." After wetting her lips, she braved his gaze and found a dark storm hovering there.

"And *you* thought it okay to keep lying to me?"

Ellis chewed the inside of her lip. Shook her head, feeling the sting of tears and hating herself for them again. She hadn't cried this much in ages, but the stress of keeping the secret and the anxiety of being so close to the man she'd admired and respected for so long . . . "I—"

"Unbelievable." He tossed the folio on the desk and started away.

"She felt you would stop working with me because I was a woman."

The storm moved back in, pressing her back against the desk. "And that's how little you thought of me? To not even to give me the chance to prove that wrong?" His gaze felt as a knife thrust into her story, her heart. "You trusted me for nearly a billion dollars of my money, but not to be man enough to partner with a woman."

"Would you have?" Ellis asked, squinting. "Because I tried

to contact you personally several times and those emails went unanswered."

"And that's how you justify lying to me?"

"No." She held up a hand. "No justification. It was wrong of me. *I* was wrong to continue the deception. But once interest awakened and sponsors started coming in . . ." She smiled, aching for him to see the wonder of it all. The beauty of what this meant. "It's happening. Your dream is coming tr—"

"Forget it." His lip curled. "I'm not doing it. I'm done. Through."

She froze. "You cannot be serious. We have the signatures. And finally, after months of negotiating and lobbying, we finally have Reighton's stamp of approval. It's done. We just have to start—"

"Nothing!" He jerked toward the door. "There's nothing to start. This is over."

"Eamon, please."

Rounding on her, he resented the way his heart cinched at the panic gouged into her face. "I will not do this again, go against my instincts. I knew you were trouble," he barked.

"Titanis." Thorsen stepped into the room, stopping Eamon's exit. "We have a problem."

Eamon nodded him out, but Thor didn't move.

"Guests are gathering for the gala. There's a guy up there. Says he's William Cramer."

"Yeh?"

"I know Cramer—dated his daughter for a couple of months." Thor pointed back up the stairs. "That's not Cramer."

Eamon's heart backfired. "Get up there with him. Stay on him. I'll have—"

Crack! Crack-crack!

Pop-pop-pop!

Crack!

Eamon jerked, arms unfolding, brow loosening as his gaze traced the ceiling. Thorsen did the same.

"M4s," Thor noted.

"Gunfire?" Ellis's stomach clenched.

"Can't get to the security hub from main access," Thor said calmly. He cleared the passage then eased forward.

"My quarters." Eamon turned to her. Motioned her out. They sandwiched Ellis, guiding her to the left, opposite end from the stairs. When they could go no farther, Eamon slid back a panel in the wall, revealing a hidden access. Thor dove in first, vanishing within the dark space. "In." Eamon nudged her inside and pushed in behind her.

She gripped the rail of a spiral staircase and as her foot hit the first step, light winked out. Breath caught in her throat, Ellis stilled.

"Move," Eamon urged from behind.

Her eyes slowly adjusted and she realized there were red emergency lights along the steps. The space constricted, tightening the breath in her lungs. Ellis hurried as fast as she could, her pulse firing fast. She took comfort in the safety of the two men with her, but the sound of more shots somewhere in the ship drilled holes in her courage.

At the top, Ellis realized there was even less space. She touched Thor's shoulders, drawing his gaze, but it was the only way to keep a proper distance between them. But Eamon crowded in and that propriety vanished. His chest pressed against her shoulders and forced her into the personal space of Thor, who flipped open a small panel. A screen sprang to life and revealed a black-and-white image.

"Clear," Thor muttered, then punched a button that pulled back the panel.

They dumped out into an enormous room, and she took a greedy draught of the conditioned air. Blue tones of the decor seemed to amplify the cool air and generous square footage. Accents of red grabbed her attention—pillows on a u-shaped leather sofa that hugged a wall. Beyond it through sliding doors loomed a king-sized bed. To her left, a large bathroom. Awareness flashed through her—Eamon's stateroom.

Eamon and Thor went into a closet, where he accessed a security pad. A few beeps and the wall glided out of sight. Racks of weapons and gear waited.

Ellis drew in a quiet breath.

Pivoting, Eamon handed her a vest. "Put it on."

Her hands trembled as she took it.

"Get back to Tariq, take Warren with you. Assess the situation," he said, tucking a clear plastic piece into his ear. "Click updates every two minutes." He rotated his wrist and glanced at the watch snugged against his inner forearm. "Sync in three . . . two . . . now."

"Done." Thor stuffed the piece into his ear as he turned to another wall.

"Wait." Eamon's terse command froze both Thor and Ellis. "Look."

The screen revealed a flurry of activity in a room. Armed men swarmed a workstation and dragged a man from behind a desk. "That's Tariq," Ellis muttered.

Thor's curse proved searing.

"Move," Eamon said as he threw himself at a panel and punched in a code.

Thor started backing out, forcing Ellis into the living room. He glanced around the stateroom, then his gaze speared past her to Eamon. "What now?"

"Back to the lower deck," Eamon said. "I'm going to find my—"

A shrieking noise blared through the ship. The speaker. "Where are you, Beast of Cape York? We have your guests, your crew, one of your security officers, and even dear old mum."

Eamon punched the back of the couch.

"You have five minutes before I provide a feast for the sharks."

CHAPTER 8

Eamon started a timer on his watch. The captor also had the security hub and the captain, which meant he had control of his boat. And his life. By the throat. Eamon mentally ran through scenarios. The *ViCross* had a speedboat and outboard docked near the pool deck. Two dive props.

Guests on the salon and main decks held at gunpoint.

He and Thor had a small arsenal. Against how many? They'd seen three take the security hub and Tariq, but to hold that many people hostage required a dozen. "We need eyes on the salon. See what we're up against." He made his way to his desk and accessed his computer. Though it powered up, he couldn't get into the system. He frowned. "Bugger."

Thor shouldered in. "What?"

"They've locked everyone out."

"So we have to get humint."

In person. Eyes on the tangos. "Yep." But how?

"I'm sorry," Warren said. "But he said he'd kill people. Aren't you going up there?"

"Not until he has to." Thor unslung the rifle he'd tossed across his back. Set it on the desk.

Eamon watched, knowing what Thor was thinking, and fisted his hands. Wished he wasn't thinking it. Angry that their captors had taken his boat without him knowing it, bringing them to their knees in minutes. "Not a good idea."

"Got a better one?" Thor dropped the clip on his pistol and racked the slide, popping out the bullet, which he caught.

Then set both on the desk before he removed the tac vest.

Eamon stood. Planted his hands on his belt. "Speedboat and outboard are the best options, if we can get the guests to the pool deck."

Thor nodded. "Assuming I'm still alive to do that." He lifted his wrist and verified their watches were in sync.

"Two clicks for yes. One for no."

"Copy that," Thor said. Took a deep breath. Then moved into the spiral staircase.

"Where's he going?"

"Lower deck. He'll come up the stairs and act like he was caught off guard."

"But they'll know who he is."

Eamon nodded. "Most likely." The tangos knew who everyone was. But how? Was the source standing right in front of him?

"What if they kill him?"

"Then I know I can't trust their word. A common theme today."

"I know you think you can't trust me, but you're wrong."

"So you've come clean about everything? You don't know anything else?" Guilt flickered through her eyes and he probed her. "Was your plan to ingratiate yourself with my mum to get these men here?"

Her eyes sprung wide? "*What*? I have nothing to do with that! I am not a violent person—I wanted to help warriors, not be one. Look, I screwed up—perpetuated a lie, but only in the hopes you'd let me work with you."

He couldn't risk it. "You're staying here."

She gaped. "You're going to leave me?"

Something tugged at the back of his brain and brought annoyance with it. "Look, we don't have time to argue this. I already know I can't trust you, so do yourself a favor and stay put. If you come out, you could end up dead."

"By you?"

"So you don't view the man holding thirty innocents, including my mum, a threat?"

"Of course I do!"

"But you only assumed *I* would kill you."

She deflated. "Because I see hatred in your eyes." More of that guilt registered in her face, and then something else. Regret? "I know you'll never forgive me for that, but—"

"No time," Eamon said. Weapon at the ready, he moved to the hidden passage and did a two-second recon to verify it was empty. He slid in, cautious, gun aimed down through the iron steps. With stealth, he cleared it and made it to the lower level. He entered a code and a steel panel slid shut. He wasn't convinced she wasn't a part of the takeover of his ship, but he wasn't certain she was either. If she got trapped, she'd need a way out. He couldn't let her into his stateroom again. She'd seen too much. Lower deck would be best. "3-1-1-3. That's the code to this door and this one only."

"Please don't leave me here." She'd gone whiter than when she'd been seasick, giving him pause. "Please."

A memory, dark and distant, called to him. A little girl . . .

No time. "I can't play protector, guess your motives or secrets, and save thirty passengers." Might be better to keep her with him, but maybe she'd shoot him in the back. He skirted her and started up the steps, glancing at his watch. Shouts rattled through the hull followed by a crack. Eamon froze, jerking to look in the direction of the salon.

Warren rushed up behind him, catching his arm. "What was that?" she gasped.

He glanced at his watch. Still had 2:15. "Our captor proving he's not patient."

"Someone just died?" Her eyes watered. "Please don't. I'm begging you. You can't leave me."

"You're a liability and a liar. You can't shoot. You don't know tactics. You are a distraction to what I have to do." But when a tear slipped free and slid down her cheek, Eamon gritted his teeth. Stepped back down. "Look, there's a better likelihood you'll live by staying here. I'll be back. I promise."

Whiplash. Straight into the past. Twenty years ago. Hiding from a kidnapper in the woods of a German forest with—

Eamon growled. He didn't need the guilt of that failure overshadowing this mission. He cut her a glare. "I need you to gut it up and do what I say. If you aren't involved in this, your best chance to stay alive is to remain here. Got it?"

Her throat processed what looked like a painful swallow. She nodded.

"Good."

"Where are you going?"

He hesitated. Why did she want to know that? There were several hidden passages and he intended to get into another to assess the situation. But even if she wasn't complicit with this attack, she didn't need to worry about him. He hustled to the top. "The code?"

Warren blinked, something crazy-familiar about the fear that trimmed her face and the way she was responding. He didn't have time to sort it out. "Code."

"I . . . 3-1-1-3."

"Who do you open it for?"

"You."

He nodded. "Not my mum, not Tariq, not even Thor."

"Why?"

"Because someone gave them the intel on my ship, and it's either someone up there or right here."

"Your mum was right—you are thickheaded." She huffed. "Lying about the complex nearly killed me. This"—she motioned upward and around—"has nothing to do with me."

"That'd be nice to believe."

"Then believe it."

Eamon gave her a long look, wondering if he could. If he did, what would it cost him?

Not worth the risk. Right now, he trusted two men: Glock

and Colt. He stepped back, keyed in his code and watched as the fireproof wall slid down between them, sealing her in.

THIS WAS JUST like Courchevel. Only it wasn't as cold. Or in the mountains. And they weren't skiing. Okay, so maybe it wasn't like it at all because this time, he'd left her alone. Ellis folded herself onto a step, grateful for the dull red glow of the emergency light that wasn't bright enough to give away the location, yet provided her a measure of comfort. Wrapping her arms around her legs, she closed her eyes. Tried to remember the Eamon she'd known then. The one who'd saved her life with a daring escape in the middle of the night. The one who peeked out from behind his barriers and nearly kissed her on the deck. Oh, glorious! But when he pulled away, the change was as visible as a physical wall, and she didn't want to hear an apology or another remonstration.

She just couldn't take it anymore. She wouldn't let him be the Beast of Cape York to her. Ever. In Courchevel, he'd become her hero. Though her parents had her declared dead, afraid the kidnappers would try again and fearful she wouldn't survive a "next time," her parents had her spirited away. She'd been badly injured that night, but she'd survived. Because of Eamon. But the world didn't know that. Eamon didn't even know.

Nobody could know still. When he'd asked what else she was hiding, her heart had tripped over the coarse tracks of her lies. She'd grown up with a new name and a new life, far removed from that one she'd been born to as Lady Victoria Ellis Rostov-Leclair, descended through her father from the Sun King, Louis XIV.

Ellis had never cared about having royal blood, just grateful to be alive. The lies had hurt her far more than they could hurt others—she had been forced to live apart from her family, watch the news detail their grief—and the Straiders'. That. That had been most cruel. She'd lost a friend, Eamon, and he grieved her supposed death. Alaina said Eamon had gone into the army because of his inability to save Ellis. She had only been six and he a much-older fifteen. If it was true, it'd be humbling.

"*It's okay, Ellis,*" *he reassured her as she clung to his shoulders and back as they climbed from the tunnel he'd dug beneath the floor while their captors were unaware. He'd used each night to do it. To save them. They'd ventured into the bitter cold of the woods and cruel bite of a Switzerland winter.* "*I won't let you die.*" *The promise dug sharply into her mind.* "*But you have to be a brave Scout now.*"

"*Dad said I make a terrible Scout,*" *she'd cried petulantly.* "*I'm a lady.*"

"*But even ladies are strong and brave,*" *he said firmly.* "*And you must be if you want to see your dad again.*"

She'd wanted to cry, but something about him made her lift her chin instead.

"*I need you to do this, Ellis. Will you? For me—for your buddy, eh?*"

Buddy. Their families had been strongly connected through their mothers. He hated her now. Trust was crucial for a friendship, and that had been decimated by the deception. She ached to blame someone else, but she must take responsibility for it. Ultimately, she made the choice to continue the lie.

Shouts reverberated through the hull of the ship.

Crack-crack! The barrage of shots followed.

Thudding feet, running.

Ellis froze, staring at the steel barrier, a harbinger of years past. Fear coiled around her and traced an icy finger down her spine where she still bore the scars of that harrowing experience. *Not there. I'm not there. Eamon saved me then. He'll save me now.*

What was happening out there? Where was Eamon? Was he okay?

She wasn't even sure how long she'd been closed in, but it was long enough that her bones were starting to ache.

Should she go out there?

Could she even remember the code?

3-1-1-3.

No. She'd broken his trust once. She wouldn't do it again if she could help it. She stared at the lone red light glaring down on her, much as Eamon had. Because he'd started to let her in. Talk with her. Smile even. Then he'd figured out about the gala.

But why would he give her the code . . . ? To test her?

Staying in this tin-can stairwell could mean her death. What if the yacht sunk?

The thought shoved the breath back up her throat. She forced herself to stay seated. Buried her face in her arms. *God, this really isn't cool, putting me in another life-or-death situation.*

Which is what Eamon did every day. So heroically that he'd earned the Victoria Cross. Of course, she'd known years ago he was a hero.

The steel door hissed out of sight, snapping Ellis to her feet. She swung herself around and stuffed herself into the shadows of the corner.

A shape flew into the passage.

The door snapped shut.

Eamon dropped hard against the stairs, gripping the pole around which the steps climbed. "Warren," came his searching growl as he stared up the steps.

She pushed forward. "Here."

He startled, turning. Then he winced, dropped against the step with a grunt.

That's when she saw the blood and gasped. "You're shot!"

"Graze." He panted, shaking his head as he sat there.

"My dad always said I wouldn't make a good Scout."

His head snapped up, brow furrowing. "What?"

She smiled. "Nothing. I just—the sight of blood . . ."

He was still staring. Frowning.

"What's wrong?"

He shook his head but that scowl remained. Then finally cleared. "All right, look. You'll need to stay here for a sec."

It was her turn to scowl. "I'm not good with confined spaces." Being locked in the crawl space . . . Wriggling through that tunnel . . .

"Well, when it means your life, you make it work. I don't know how long. Just stay here until I come back."

"Why?" Why had he come back to tell her to stay? "What are you planning?"

He dropped his gaze. Glanced at the graze across his shoulder. "I'm going to give them what they want."

It took her a second to realize his meaning. *"What—no!"*

"We have a plan. So, just stay put."

"Eamon—"

"Non-negotiable. Stay." He pulled something from his pant pocket. Reached for her, with a bloodied hand. "Your arm."

She held it out and he strapped on a watch. "The stem allows clicks. Two for yes, once for no." He held up a bud. "In your ear. You'll hear what's going on. No voice communication, understood?"

Mute, she nodded, realizing he still had his. Was this him trusting her?

"Thor and I have one."

"What about Tariq?"

Eamon's jaw muscle jounced. "Remember. Stay here. No matter how long. I will be back."

Why didn't he answer about Tariq? Was that who'd been killed earlier? Panic pounded through her breast. "Eamon, please. You're scaring me. No—I'm terrified."

"Good. So am I."

"That is not comforting."

"Not meant to be." He pushed to his feet and towered over her. "It's not a game. I want you to understand the danger if you leave this hidden access." He pointed toward the ceiling. "He's playing for keeps." Eamon's gaze darkened. "So am I."

There was a thought. A dangerous one. A familiar one. Both past and present colliding in this moment. She didn't want to ask, but it slipped past her control. "What if you don't come back?"

He touched her cheek. And she leaned into it, surprised. Anxious. Desperate to not be separated from him. Belatedly, she realized he'd entered the key code. The door whooshed open and it seemed to snatch him into the passage. Away from her, hauling her hope with it.

He pivoted and walked down the hall with all ease and confidence.

Her brain caught up with actions. Ellis threw herself at the opening. "Eamon!" It snapped shut. She crumpled against it, nearly catching her fingers. She palmed it, tears freeing themselves, knowing what was he was going to do. Terrified he wouldn't come back because Eamon planned to sacrifice himself.

She turned her tears and gaze to the keypad.

CHAPTER 9

Glock placed behind the vase in the grand foyer, Eamon held his hands out to each side and rounded the corner to the salon. Two guards in kit and armed with M4s brought those weapons to bear when they spotted him.

He stopped, not wanting to eat lead before he could get in the salon.

As one flipped open the door, the other trained the weapon on him and called over his shoulder to the guy in charge. He wagged the muzzle at Eamon, motioning him inside.

"You cost a man his life," the boss said, his voice nearly amused. He stood maybe five-ten, maybe five-eleven. Graying blond hair. His bearing bespoke military. Career maybe. But definitely special operations. And the accent American.

"His blood is not on my hands. You killed him with two minutes fifteen to spare," Eamon said, surreptitiously taking the pulse of the crowd. Nervous. Scared. Thor was sitting apart from the others with Eamon's mum. That told him two things: these men were very well-informed, and the target was very specific—Eamon.

"You are wrong, Straider. Your man here made it in under two minutes, so I had only to surmise that you were attempting to defy me. You cost Tariq's blood," he said motioning to the body on the floor. "Now, where is the princess?"

Eamon frowned.

"Come. You can't think I don't know about Hayley Warren."

"She got sea sick. Sent her back to land. She's a liar anyway. Why would I want her on my boat?"

The man clicked his tongue. "Think more carefully before endangering the lives of your guests, Mr. Straider. Or should I say, Corporal?"

Were they getting to the crux of things now with the mention of his rank? Was the man jealous of Eamon's notoriety? Or was there something deeper here?

"What do you want?" Eamon asked.

"I have what I want—you."

As he'd expected. "Then let them go."

A crinkling smile pinched the man's eyes. "That'd be too easy." He moved to the main table and leaned back against it, dangling a Glock as casually as one might a book. "And that would also mean I wouldn't have the immense pleasure of exposing you for the fraud you are."

"Then you *don't* have what you want."

Anger glinted in the man's eyes, but the smile parked on his stubbled jaw never wavered. "Do you know who I am, Corporal Straider?"

"A man with a vendetta."

An eyebrow winged up as he cocked his head. "On this we can agree." He scratched his jaw. "But more specifically, I am the brother of a man you killed."

Eamon flipped through his mental files. "My kills are isolated to terrorists. Unless your brother—"

"My brother," the man growled, coming alive and off the table, "was one of the finest soldiers to have existed. He followed you into combat, relied on intel you provided, and came home in a box."

There were two men who fit that description. One was Hispanic. The other—"Niehauer."

The man smirked. "Guilt prods your memory, does it,

Corporal Straider?"

"Guilt? No. Regret? Absolutely. For every man lost."

"Cory wasn't 'every man,' Cory was my little brother," he said, with no trace now of that implacable smile. "I was afraid I'd have to kill dear old mom to make my point. To win."

"Killing isn't winning. Nobody else has to die." He thought of Hayley in the stairwell. "Just—"

"Oh, that is simply not true," Niehauer corrected. "And you are *not* in control. Don't pretend you are or try to take it. That'd be disastrous. The famed Beast of Cape York, hero of Melbourne, wearer of the Victoria Cross—times two, would then add twenty-eight more lives to his kill sheet." Again, Niehauer tilted his head at Eamon. "Have you such an appetite for control that you would risk their lives?"

"No."

Nodding, Niehauer motioned to one of his guards, who dragged a chair across the deck and planted it in the middle of the room. The man stood in challenge, his silver throat mic more advanced than the rest. Was he higher up the food chain than the other grunts?

"Sit," Silver growled.

Eamon looked to Niehauer as he settled on the cushioned seat. "I get to die sitting down?" He wasn't tied. Even if they'd bound his hands and feet, the chair wasn't secured. Didn't Niehauer have a brain? Or maybe he did. And he wanted Eamon to make that mistake. Try to attack him and find himself with two extra holes in his head.

"Position doesn't matter. End result does." Niehauer hefted his weapon and pushed off the table. "Have you wondered why I chose this time?"

Eamon shrugged. "As good as any."

"Not quite true, but close enough." He waved the gun toward Tariq's body. "Surprised you didn't catch on to this, though. Tariq was pretty easy to buy." He stalked the guests, pacing like a caged animal. "You see, it was very kind of you to have such a grand event, invite members of your Parliament, and those with a voice in the special operations command."

Eamon's muscles constricted. Reighton.

"Because it was one man who advocated for your involvement and leadership, an experiment to see what could be learned, how soldiers could be cross trained. And it was you, under his authorization, that put you in command of my brother."

"I wasn't in command."

Bending toward a cluster of people, Niehauer reached past two women and grabbed Reighton by the lapels and dragged him to his feet. "Semantics, Straider. Suh-man-ticks." He pitched the nobleman at Eamon's feet.

The former SAS officer struggled back to his feet in defiance, but the guards were swift. Landed a blow to his stomach. Whacked the back of his knees with the M4 and sent Reighton back to the floor. He braced against the marble to stop from face-planting. The guard flashed in, holding him there.

"Cory was one of the best soldiers I worked with," Eamon said, feeling the strain of desperation to protect Reighton. "He wouldn't have wanted this."

"No, what my brother wanted was to get married—"

"Rachel."

Niehauer glowered. "*Don't*," he growled. "Don't act like you cared about him."

"They were going to get married," Eamon persisted. "Rachel was pregnant—"

"Cory's son is *fatherless*. Is that what you were going to say next? Was it?" Niehauer shouted. "I dare you." He aimed his weapon at Reighton's head. "Say it or he dies."

Eamon stilled. Clamped his jaw tight.

"Say it!" Niehauer roared. His hand trembled as much as his body. Rage driving him. Curling his finger around the trigger well. The weapon wavering. If he pulled it, that bullet could go wild.

Though Eamon knew no matter what he did or said, Reighton was as good as dead, if there was even the smallest hope that he could save the man's life, he'd do it. "Co—"

Crack!

Eamon came up out of the chair. Launched at Niehauer, but found himself hauled backward, two guards manifesting out of thin air. Two more rushing in with weapons. He anticipated the fire of being shot again. Expected it.

"No no no!" Niehauer hollered, holding his hands out to the incoming shooters.

The guards slammed Eamon back against the chair. And with it the sickening awareness that he had caused yet another man to die. The cost had been too high. But it'd provided proof—Niehauer didn't want him dead *yet*. But this man was out-of-his-skull bloodthirsty.

"This would disgust Cory!" Eamon shouted as he struggled against them until he felt the press of steel at his temple. He stilled, staring at the body spilling life at his feet.

"Who's next, Corporal Straider? You do know that I have men hunting down the princess." He bent forward, staring into Eamon's eyes. "You know that, right?"

This was too much like the kidnapping nearly twenty years ago with little Ellis. At fifteen, he'd been scared, terrified—with no skills to speak of, yet he'd done what he could. This time, he had to do better. He *wouldn't* let Warren down as he had Ellis. Couldn't fail her the way he had Niehauer and Raptor team.

And this man, this man wanted to weigh Eamon down with more deaths on his conscience. Threatened each of them. Threatened Warren. Something fiery crawled through Eamon's veins. Fury coiled around his chest, constricting his restraint. His mind had a will of its own. He threw his head forward, cracking it against Niehauer's skull.

The man stumbled back with a flurry of searing curses.

Silver lunged in, driving a hard right straight into Eamon's face. It threw him backward, flipped the chair. Then Silver drove his boot into Eamon's gut. Bile rose with the explosion of pain. He didn't think a rib cracked but close.

"Enough!" Niehauer yelled. "Sit him up."

His defiance and attitude were working—distracting them. Giving Thor the needed time to inform the guests. To ready them. Though Tariq had betrayed him by providing Niehauer access to the *ViCross* and its manifest, he'd paid with his life. But thankfully, it seemed he hadn't informed him of the hidden passages. But what if he had? What if Niehauer was just toying with him.

"Ah, you do know we're closing in on her. And you're afraid. Heard you even kissed this one, too. Is that a pattern? Get in bed with them and betray your team?"

Heat streaked through Eamon, but he would not be baited. "What's your goal, Niehauer? Shoot every passenger at my feet? Is that supposed to bring meaning to Cory's death?"

The butt of the Glock flew at Eamon's face. Though he lifted a hand to block, he was too late. Pain cracked his temple. Scored his thoughts. His vision blurred. Even as he pulled himself straight, Eamon felt the swelling. Warmth sliding down his face.

Niehauer hissed. "See? You're ruining my plan, Corporal Straider. We are messing up the Beast of Cape York's face—well, more than it already is with that hideous scar."

In his periphery, Eamon noticed a camera being set up. "Better a hideous scar than a black heart."

"You don't think you have a black heart? How can you be warrior and not know the color of your own heart?" Niehauer leaned back and laughed. Motioned around the salon, to Tariq's body in the corner and to where they'd removed Reighton's. "I thought it was pretty obvious. No? Do we need another demonstration?" He started toward the guests again.

"No wonder Cory couldn't stand you."

Niehauer spun back. Stormed toward Eamon. "What did you say?"

"He told me once that you scared him. That he wasn't sure what to do. He'd considered going to your CO."

With a howl, Niehauer struck him with the Glock. Again. Again. Eamon cowered beneath the blows, glad it was him taking the hits. Not someone else. Not someone else eating lead. Another death on his conscience.

Blood sliding down his face and glancing across his tongue, eyes swelling, Eamon bent away. Saw something in the grand foyer. Movement. His heart hitched when the shape coalesced into the trim figure of Hayley Warren. *No!*

"Boss!" Silver shouted. "The girl!"

"Get her!"

CHAPTER 10

Panicked and in a rage of his own, Eamon punched upward. Let loose the punches he'd withheld. It took four well-placed strikes to neutralize the guard who came at him first. Elbow to the gut. Back fist to the nose. Knife-hand to the throat. When the guy wheeled back, clutching his neck and wheezing for air, Eamon stepped in. Drove his fist into his face. Gray matter pushed into his skull. He crumpled, moaning. Incapacitated. Dead soon enough.

A shorter, stockier guard came at him with the AR15. Sidestepping as the guy fired off a few rounds, Eamon grabbed the barrel. Pulled it and the man into his fist. The man stumbled back, releasing the weapon. Now in control of the weapon, he flipped it and squeezed off a controlled burst, the guard neutralized.

Eamon turned toward Niehauer. He was gone. And the door to the foyer was sliding closed. Crap. Niehauer, Silver, and another guard were missing. He spun toward the access panel.

"They've got another half-dozen onboard," Thor announced as he guided guests into the passage that would lead down to the lower deck. There, they'd slip into another and get to the pool deck, where they'd launch the speed boat. "Go! They'll slice and dice her."

Eamon nodded, trotting backward. He pointed to his man, knowing Thor's loyalty rivaled his own. "Stick to the plan. Get them out of here."

Thor hesitated then finally gave a nod.

His mum straightened in his view. "Eamon, save her. She's not who you think she is. Don't let her die this time."

This time? What did that mean? Eamon rolled around, snatched up stocky's M4 and handgun. Moving toward the grand foyer, he dropped the mags to verify the ammo, then slapped them back in and chambered rounds. He eased open the door with his shoulder, staring down the sights into the passage. Left. Right. Too quiet up here, so she must've led them below. He hurried to the stairs and used the wall to guide him down. Rounding corners were tricky, so he pulled the weapon firm against his shoulder. Flashed out. *Clear.* He hustled down the four steps.

Since the passage was on the left, giving a shooter a perfect line of sight, he skirted it and moved to the opposite wall. Hated the time it took to clear the passage but rushing would get him killed. Still too quiet. Nerves thrummed. Quiet meant Niehauer could hole up in a stateroom with Warren. Ambush him.

He cursed the futility of the half-dozen VIP quarters on this deck and how long it'd take to clear them. Crouching he verified the juncture was clear, and moved into the gangway. Shouldering the wall by the first door, he mentally mapped the room, taking no more than a couple of seconds to prepare himself. Then he stepped back and slammed his heel into the door. It flung backward. Boot on the floor, he snapped up the weapon. Rushed in. Pied right and left in a sweeping motion. Hurried toward the bathroom. Cleared it. Raced back to the passage for the next quarters, knowing each door could be the last one he opened.

At the second, he braced—Warren's stateroom. He breathed out. Checked the knob. Unlocked. He flicked it open. Rushed in, neurons firing, aligning some things. Misaligning others. Even as he cleared it, Eamon wondered at the "too perfect" back history. What would that have to do with her impersonating Vic Toriael? He hesitated, the revelation too heady to keep moving. The back history suggested she wasn't who she claimed to be. Two pieces of the puzzle that didn't connect. And his mum's cryptic comment about letting her die *this time* . . .?

His gaze dropped on something glittering on the floor. Eyes hitting the door, he bent and dragged a finger over it. A necklace. He lifted it and rose, only dropping his gaze for a second. Elaborate scrollwork supported an emerald within a script E.

E?

Crack! Pop! Pop!

Eamon whipped around, his gaze dropping. Shots were coming from the lower deck. Crap! That was where Thor should be by now, ferrying the guests to the boat and outboard. Tucking the necklace into his pocket, Eamon turned into the stairwell and made quick work of clearing it. With care, he angled around a corner.

The wall exploded at him. Spit splintered pieces at his face. He jerked back, pulse jammed. Slammed against the wall and pulled up the M4. He angled out, sighting the target. Kneeling at the entrance to the gangway, the man was in a prime spot to take Eamon down.

Had to force his way down. Eamon took a second to mentally prepare himself. Hefted the weapon. Stalked forward, firing in four-shot bursts. Peppering the man. Saw him go down.

An arm hooked Eamon's throat. In that split-second, he realized he hadn't cleared the two-foot alcove to the right of the stairs. The man choke-holding him had to be tall to secure Eamon and haul him to his toes. In a painfully slow second, a serrated blade slid into view.

Knew what the man intended.

Eamon shoved backward, pinning the man into the corner to limit his options. He arched his back, again slamming the man against the wall while holding his hand-wielding knife. With his large hands, gripping it tight proved easy. He pinched his thumb into the soft spot between the man's thumb and finger. Flexed the hand backward with a resounding crack. He heard the blade drop.

Sharp, searing pain stabbed Eamon's left leg. It buckled. A second knife! Eamon elbowed the man's gut. Felt the familiar hard shape of a gun in a side holster. When the man doubled and Eamon threw a back-fist into his nose, he used his other hand to snatch the man's holstered weapon. He pitched himself forward and twisted around, bringing the gun to bear. Fired. Once. Twice. Three times.

The man lurched at him and landed on Eamon. They crashed into the wall, pain scoring his leg and the back of his skull. When his attacker didn't move, Eamon dragged himself free. Made quick work of relieving the guard of the knives and weapons, then pulled himself against the wall. He inspected the weapons, checked ammo as he scanned the gangway, the stairs up, the stairs down. The end of the passage to the hidden access panel.

Warren.

His mum's pleading words assailed him—*save her!*

Where was she? Had she made it back safely? He tore off a strip of material from the edge of his shirt and tied it around the knife wound, growling through the pain. He should check for Warren. Hauling himself up, wincing at the wound, he kept his weapon and mind ready as he hobbled down the passage. Halfway down, he heard a scream. Then gunfire.

"C'MON!"

Ellis stared across the pool, disbelieving the sight—guests snaking through a door, quickly, quietly. Thorsen stood there, motioning her toward them. "Move! Now!"

Alaina was there, too, waving her. "Ellis, hurry!"

She scurried across the deck and through the door. Guests were being loaded onto a blue and gray speedboat that sat on skis that would lower it to the surface. Alaina, who had already seated herself, came to her feet. "Here."

Ellis glanced around the half-dozen people boarding ahead of her and realized he wasn't here yet. "Where's Eamon?"

Holding a woman's hand and assisting her onto the boat, Thor shrugged. "Keeping them distracted."

She glanced back to the door. Peered through it across the pool to the glass doors that afforded only the slightest view of the last of the stairs. "What if he's in trouble?"

"He'll get out of it." Thor nodded her into the boat. "Get on board."

"I have to help him."

He scoffed. "He doesn't need your help."

"We can't leave him. How can you—he's your boss, right?"

"I work for him. And he gave me orders." His hazel eyes flashed. "These people are my responsibility. Staving off Niehauer is his."

She'd been right. Eamon intended to sacrifice himself.

And he'd told her to wait. But he saw her when she'd intentionally drawn the attention of the shooters. He'd seen her, so he'd know she wasn't in that hidden stairwell. "He saw me, right? He knows I'm not—"

"Barton, take her down," Thor shouted, looking past her to the black rubber boat that had about ten people on it. "Head to the coordinates I gave you."

The man saluted and hit the button. A hydraulic lift lowered the outboard into the water. Roaring to life, the engine churned the waters, sending a foamy wake crashing against the skids that held the speed boat. It rocked.

Within seconds, the rear bay door slid up, and the

outboard shot out of the yacht and away a good hundred feet or more. It banked a hard left and never slowed.

"Warren. *Now*!"

Ellis spun back to Thorsen. Looked to Alaina, whose worried gaze had locked onto the door. Then back to the pool. *Eamon* . . .

"You're no help to him. You're a liability," came Thor's voice, more distant. He'd moved onto the boat. He stood at the wheel. "Don't do it, Warren. He wouldn't want you to."

"Help!" Alaina yelped, reaching for a man, who'd bent forward, clutching his chest. "He's having a heart attack!"

Thor started. Jerked to Ellis. "Med kit! On the wall."

Ellis looked where he pointed—across the pool room—and saw the white box with a red cross mounted on the wall. She sprinted to it, flicked free the first two braces that had it. But the third one wouldn't unlock. "Come on," she muttered, jiggling the partially rusted metal. It finally surrendered, but not before biting into her finger. She hissed and turned—and froze.

Three armed men were in the passage. Shouts and shots ensued with someone out of sight. Eamon. Had to be. Spurred by the thoughts, Ellis pressed herself against the wall. As if she could sink into it. Told herself to breathe. Stay put.

The glass door shattered. A man stumbled backward, heel catching on the frame and pitched onto his back. What if they spotted her? Used her against Eamon? *You're a liability!* And she would be if she didn't hide.

Slinking along the wall, Ellis moved to an open door, the one she'd seen the guests emerge from. She tucked herself through it and slid the door closed.

ONE OF HIS mother's guests lay dead on the floor. Beyond the dead man, the others were cramming into the speedboat.

Just then, two men emerged from the passage, rushing toward the dock room.

Eamon rushed through the emptiness of the door whose glass crunched beneath his boots—movement in his periphery forced him to look but nothing was there. He yanked open the supply room door and used it for cover as he took his first shot, felling the man who'd started firing at the guests.

Having neutralized him, Eamon aimed at the second, who dropped to a knee, but rolled and brought his weapon up.

Eamon fired again.

The wall spit at him, a bullet having thudded into the wall. He jerked back and heard an exchange of weapons' fire. When he looked back, the third was down—compliments of Thor.

Eamon jogged across to the speed boat.

"Haven't seen Niehauer," Thor said as the boat was lowering. "And Warren went back."

That stopped Eamon. "What?"

"She was getting the med kit when they came in."

He pivoted, remembering what he'd seen—that panel shutting.

The speed boat was in the water. The engine started, a wake writhing.

The plan had been simple: Get off the ship. Get the civvies to safety. Not get killed.

If he didn't go with Thor and his mum, he still had options: dive props, swimming to safety, or even fighting it out. Which had a low chance of survival with him wounded. While Niehauer's men were tough, they weren't invincible.

Then again, neither am I.

"I could wait—or you could go and I'll stay."

"Eamon, you have to know," his mum said, scrambling toward him, over the legs of the other guests. "Eamon, listen to me."

"Mum, stop. Stay—"

"I have to tell you because she won't—*can't* tell you herself." Huffing, his mum reached the port side. "You must listen to me."

"We don't have time—"

"She—" Scowling, she reached for him and he went to a knee, frowning. She clutched his arm and tugged him closer. "Eamon, she's Ellis."

He frowned. Scoffed. "Mum." He grieved what she'd been through in the last hour, knew it'd addled her. "You're in shock. Ellis died twenty—"

"No. She didn't."

His heart misfired, remembering the wound that pierced her back and stomach. All the blood in the snow. "She did. I was—"

"Pietr and Marie feared for her safety, so they told the world she'd died."

Searching her face for confusion from a blow or the shock of the terrorists who'd killed people in front of her gave him no proof. A joke then? But it was there. Dead set serious. "I . . . no."

"Find her, Eamon!"

Shouts came from the stairs. More guns.

Eamon shoved to his feet. Spotted shadows in the passage. He jerked to Thor. "Go!"

"But—"

"*Go!*" he threw over his shoulder as he sprinted through the door, hauling it closed behind him. He couldn't get to the access panel without exposing Warren—*Ellis?*—so he ran to the other deep-end supply closet. Tucked himself in with the antiseptic and chlorine smells. Left himself a sliver of an opening so he could hear and exit without betraying his position. Once the person left the pool deck, he'd retrieve Warren from the hidden access and get off the ship.

In the shroud of darkness, he listened. Heard the crunch of glass doors opening. Heard footsteps and muttering as they wandered toward the dive bay.

His mind wandered, too. Was Warren actually Ellis? Why? Why would they let him believe she'd died? But . . . *Bugger!* It fit. It all fit. The too-perfect-backstory. His mum's protective inclusion of her.

"Negative visual on the guests," came the man's voice, snapping Eamon back to the real and present danger. Apparently he was giving a sitrep via his coms. "Bay is empty." The voice grew louder, his steps closer. "Negative on Straider."

Two others headed through the broken glass doors, probably going topside while the third continued the search.

As Eamon stood in the darkness, the unmistakable sound of the engines opening up reached him. He hesitated, glancing at the floor, feeling the vibration climbing up from engine room. Why was Niehauer increasing speed?

The speedboat. Niehauer was going after the speedboat.

Light shifted in the sliver of space.

Nerves thrumming, Eamon stared at the shadow formed by the tango in front of the door. The distraction of the engines' roar had concealed the man's approach. Palpable tension reached through the thin barrier and clawed at him.

Eamon shifted. Caught sight of the man angling sideways. Though he couldn't see the weapon he held, Eamon could imagine it from his stance. The door would block shots because the appointments on the pool deck were heavy duty since they were partially exposed to the elements. But if the man opened it, Eamon would be a fish in a barrel.

Stepping back, he eyed the barrier. Then drove his heel into door.

Crack!

Oof!

Eamon launched out, hearing the gun clatter to the deck. He dove right into the man's gut. The man stumbled. Screamed and fought for purchase. Eamon dug in. Shoved with his legs and shoulder. They went airborne. And he carried the man into the deep end.

CHAPTER 11

Sucking in a hard breath, Ellis shoved out of the hidden passage. Thanks to the security feed, she'd seen Eamon go into the pool with the guy. She'd watched. And waited. And waited.

But they hadn't come up.

Red bloomed through the water, pulling her closer. Closer... Hedging in until she could see dark forms at the bottom. Huddled. Tangled. Unmoving.

Heart in her throat, she considered diving in. She was no lifeguard, but... *He's going to die because of me!* Ellis kicked off her shoes. Removed her tac vest and tossed it aside. She stepped to the pool.

Water erupted, vomiting Eamon to the surface.

With a yelp strangled by relief and fright, Ellis went to her knees, reaching for him. Poseidon returned. Huffing, he swam to the side and grabbed the ledge, breathing hard.

"Eamon!"

He snapped a look at her, the same startled one he'd given her two days ago. But then his gaze darkened, grew more intense as he stared. Hard. What was that about?

Lips thinned, he hauled himself onto the deck, his clothes plastered to his body. He bent and drew in a breath then let it out.

She glanced at the water, swirling with red—blood. "Are you okay?" she asked.

Frowns seemed to be his signature. He followed her gaze

and shook his head. "Not mine."

"You were under for a long time."

"C'mon," he said, guiding her toward a panel he slid back.

As he accessed it, she stuffed on her shoes, surprised when another panel popped open, revealing a small arsenal. "How many hidden places do you have?" she asked, surprised and relieved at the same time.

He ignored her question and strapped a weapon to his right thigh. Slung one around his shoulder. A couple of knives. Then he was moving. Picking up his pace, he made his way out of the pool, down the darkened hall to another door.

"Where are we going?"

He dribbled water, leaving puddles she had to avoid so she didn't slip. "Have to shut down the engines." The approached a door marked CREW ONLY.

"Why?"

"He's going after the boats. Won't reach them—*ViCross*'s top speed is twelve knots, but he can get close enough to shoot at or destroy them." He punched in a code and shoved through a heavy steel hatch, holding it open as she ducked through.

"Why would he kill them?" she shouted over the roar of the engines. Hesitating, she wasn't sure where to go or what to do with herself, so she stepped aside, leaving room for him to pass and lead.

After locking the door, Eamon pivoted and leaned in. His mouth brushed her ear. "No witnesses."

Though she could tell he hollered it, the words came like a whisper amid the din . . . a warm, teasing whisper. Which was ridiculous considering their situation.

He strode down the steel gangway that gleamed and shone, surprisingly clean in a place she expected to find grease, oil, and grime. A cutout in the gangway dropped a steep set of stairs. Eamon grabbed the rails and hoisted himself into the yawning gap, sliding down as if he'd done it a thousand times.

Ellis took the slower, safer route of hurrying down the steel steps, afraid her wet shoes would send her flying onto her backside. At the bottom, she found herself closed in, unable to hear anything or see Eamon. Where had he gone? She peered through the wall of components and piping, stunned at the enormity of the place. Down a bit, she spied his dark shirt. Rounded the corner and hurried after him. He was bent over a waist-high instrument panel. Stepped back. Swiped a hand down his mouth and jaw.

"What?" she asked, but the noise swallowed her question. She stepped closer.

Eamon's stiff expression fell on her. His lips thinned. He glanced back at the panel, then grabbed her arm. Drew her back the direction they'd come to the yawning opening. He pointed to the stairs. "Wait by the hatch," he shouted.

There was something terrible in his expression. In his terse movements. His demand she go to the hatch. Pain. Grief. Hardcore resolve. How those things spoke to her, climbed out from behind his barriers, she didn't know. "What're you doing?"

"Go!"

Though she hesitated, something in his dark expression sent her back to the hatch in frightened obedience.

THERE WAS NO other way. And though he'd already set his course, Eamon stood at the network of stainless steel piping clustered on the wall, some treading up above deck, some below. If he did this . . . it'd mean losing . . . everything.

His home. His business. His haven.

He stepped back, covering his mouth. Steeling himself. There was no other way. They were speeding after the guests. Running a hand down the back of his neck, he lifted the

KABAR from its sheath. Tightened his grip as he drew the flint stone out of his pocket.

God . . . this is cruel.

He hadn't even wanted people on his boat.

Squatting, he aimed the KABAR at the lower pipe. Struck it and withdrew his knife. Watched as the liquid spewed from the pipe, spilling onto the deck.

Not too late to—

To what? They were gaining on his mum and dad. Thor. The innocents.

They just had to come on his boat and mess everything up, didn't they?

Eamon pushed to his feet, watching the puddle quickly grow. He backed up and turned the red rag from a rail. Grief pierced him as struck steel against flint. A spark leapt from them. He did it again. And again, sending his anger into the sparks that latched onto the rag. With a poof, the fire took.

The flames flickered and ravenously crawled through the cloth. He eyed the path of the fuel reaching for him. Maybe he'd just do like old times and go down with the ship.

Don't be morose. Or stupid.

He didn't want to die. The thought surprised him. He'd wished for it many times since the mission that killed Cory Niehauer. Marred him for life.

Behind him, he heard Warren's shout. No, Ellis's shout.

Right. So long, ViCross.

Launching himself backward, Eamon tossed the rag at the fuel. A whistle shot through the air. Gaping silence punched him. Then it came. The deafening roar.

CHAPTER 12

A CURTAIN OF fire shot upward. Mesmerizing. Beautiful. Angry.

Ellis sucked in her shock, stepping back, shoulders banging against the hatch. Pulse pounding, she panicked. "Eamon!"

He flew around the corner. Sailed up the steps like they weren't there. Fire chased him and a slick river of liquid—*gas!!*—across the deck. He waved her back, his face contorted. "Go go go!"

Terrified, she whirled. Stumbled, gaze locked onto the steel door that separated the engine room from the launch bay. Eamon plowed into her, hooking her underarms. Propelling her onward. She scrambled for purchase, mind and heart screaming. Terrified.

He threw them at the door. Opened it. Pitched her through and hopped out, slamming the door behind them. "Bay! Go!" He locked it. Stabbed a knife into the keypad.

"What did you do?" she breathed, disbelief whispering through her as she staggered toward the bay.

Eamon pushed her on. "In the water."

"What?"

He was moving. All action. No talk. Ran to a corner. Grabbed some gear. Then drew alongside a long black thing that looked like a black jet ski. He motioned her forward. Robotically, frozen by the terror of what was happening, Ellis went to him.

He slid a mask over her face, adjusted straps at the side of her face. Threaded her arms through a holster-like space. "Take a deep breath."

Was he kidding? She eyed him.

He nodded. "Do it!"

Crack! Boom! The sound of something crashing against steel else startled her, sent a tremor racing below her feet.

She gripped his wrist. "I'm scared."

He cupped her face. "Scared or dead. Your choice."

She sucked in a breath. "That doesn't help," she said, tears pushing past her iron barriers.

"Maybe, but it got you to breathe."

She twitched at that, watching as he donned his own mask. But something caught her. Hauled her backward against a solid mass.

Eamon jerked and snatched up a weapon. "Let her go!"

Thick pillars of smoke coiled around them.

"Not happening! You can't escape this. You cost my brother his life, and it's time for you to pay."

"Then let me pay," Eamon shouted, holding his hands out. "I'm here. Let her go."

"But she means something to you. As Cory did to me."

Ellis stared at Eamon, trying to read what he wanted her to do. But when the gun swung toward her head, she froze. Snapped her gaze back to Eamon.

Who was a blur of fury and action.

In a blink, he'd moved from three feet away to crashing into them. Pitched sideways by a thrust of Eamon's right hand, Ellis stumbled. Lost her balance. Alarm speared her, knowing the bay was right there. The skid. The deck vanished beneath her feet. She dropped. Crashed onto the prop that looked like a giant black sled with two fans at the back. She bent into the scooped front and grabbed on, trying to steady herself. Her ankle slipped. Caught. She wrenched it but didn't care, her gaze springing upward to where Eamon and the man wrestled.

Niehauer rolled. Fire and smoke chased them, but Eamon

was bigger. He pounded a punch, but Niehauer blocked. Threw a hard right at Eamon, who caught it, twisted the man's hand around. Though she couldn't hear the crack, she knew one had happened. Niehauer's face contorted in pain. He stumbled backward. Eamon planted a boot in his chest. Fired off a round from a weapon he'd snatched from a leg holster.

Then Eamon was coming at her.

Ellis did the only she could think of. She straddled the prop. Eamon threw himself down behind her with a thud.

Crack! Boom!

Fire snaked along the roof, eating through the ship like a ravenous demon. The sight pushed her down. Chest pressing hers to the prop, Eamon placed her hands on the bars at the front and squeezed.

Sparks flew off the prop—bullets pinging off the nose, not far from its propeller and Eamon jerked. Smoke filled the launch bay, chasing them into the water. The craft thrummed beneath her, yet when he steered them between the boat skids, the craft dropped. A strangled yelp lobbed in her throat as water swallowed them whole and they plummeted.

CHAPTER 13

BLAZE OF GLORY was not how he imagined his home tonight. Eamon sped the dive prop away from the *ViCross* in a bloom of unnatural light as the fire he'd started ate through the hull and lit the night. Though he had oxygen, he wasn't sure he could breathe after torching his home, his livelihood, his existence. And then there was the small matter of the bullet that struck him as they dived. It hadn't come out the front, which meant he had lead in him.

He monitored their depth before leveling off and navigating toward shore. It was bad enough having to burn down his home, but seeing the fear in her eyes, her shock-riddled movements. Her terror when he'd said to get in the water had nearly undone him. Brought back too many memories.

He'd thought he'd failed her twenty years ago. But she was here, straddling the prop in front of him. The sweet little girl was replaced with an intelligent, beautiful woman. As the thoughts hit him, he grew more aware of her shape beneath him.

Steer straight, Straider.

Twenty years ago, she'd trusted him, followed him. Same was true now—she hadn't screamed or demanded information. She'd done what was necessary without complaint or too many questions.

Even now, he felt her terror in the way she clung to the craft, her limbs trembling from the cold and tense muscles. To reassure her, he placed a hand over hers on the handle.

Darkness slowly devoured them as they put distance between him and the *ViCross*.

What was left of the ol' girl.

The temperature of the water changed as they neared the shore ten minutes later. Seaweed and sea life slid along his legs and arms. He guided the prop up as the radar showed them gaining the shore. A klick out, they broke the surface. Eamon eased off her spine, giving her room as he steered in a little closer.

The moon glittered on the interspersed water. When they came up on the marshes, he did his best to negotiate them, but finally gave up after about five minutes. He slid off, walking the craft in, letting Ellis stay onboard. Left hand on the control of the prop, he cupped his side with the other.

"Is this Cape York?" she asked.

"No," he said quietly. "It's east of us. We cruised the Gulf of Carpentaria the last two days. We're off the coast of Northern Territory now." He sludged onward, each step pulsing warmth down his side. A few steps more the marsh became impassable. Eamon backed them out and redirected around, trying to keep them moving south, but the area was not cooperating.

"Should I get off?" she finally asked.

He wouldn't tell her about the crocs that infested these waters. "When we get to shore." It was strange. Now that she was Ellis again, that protective instinct went into overdrive. Or was it the soft, round face and lips that drew him into a near-kiss that had done that?

Moonlight offered little light or warmth at this time of night. He heard a noise behind them: sloshing water. Couldn't be a croc—they were stealthy, especially when stalking prey. Just keep moving. Closer to shore. Closer to safety.

"How long before they come looking for us—help, I mean?"

"Once Thor reaches safety, he'll send help."

"How long will that take?"

"Depends on how fast he gets there." And if they don't have engine trouble or if Niehauer shot their fuel lines or the entire boat. That was the thing of it. He didn't know. Couldn't know. All he could know was right here. Him. Her. This marshy stretch.

"Are you mad at me?"

Eamon started. Glanced at her. "No." It was strange, weird how he suddenly didn't want to be the Beast of Cape York. Ellis Rostov-Leclair had a piece of his heart because of the twenty years he'd believed her dead. To know that was her sitting there, staring at him, depending on him, Eamon loosened his grip on the anger he'd felt over her deception. "Anyway, it'd be trivial in light of our current situation."

"What is our current situation? And please—no more platitudes. Be honest with me. I can handle it."

"You who'd make a bad Scout?"

"I might not be good at survival skills, making a fire with a hair pin, or eating worms, but I am made of pretty strong stuff, I'm told."

She was. He'd seen it. Eamon held her gaze, face awash in moonlight. "We are alive. That's our situation."

"Why are you doing that?"

"What?"

"*Not* telling me things. I feel like you're hiding the bad things from me."

"I'm focusing on facts, what we can control."

She gave a breathy laugh. "That little?"

"No sense in getting bothered by the what ifs," he said, eying the subtle glow ahead of the beach head. "Be prepared. Eyes out. Expect trouble. And you won't be caught off guard."

"You make me feel like a schoolgirl." She motioned to the sea, to the lands. "The way you did all that—you killed men, fought men, sank your own ship . . . and you're guiding this floaty with me—"

"Floaty?" he kept her talking to distract her, but he also lowered his voice. Slowed his movements so they weren't sloshing. "Dive propulsion vehicle. Dive prop."

"Whatever it is, you're just moving through this insanity as if it's a walk in the park."

Again, he eyed the water. "You're innocent of trials and combat. That doesn't make you a child. It makes you... normal."

"Do you regret it?"

He glanced at her. "What?"

"Being a commando?"

"Nope. If anything, I regret walking away." The swish came again. Closer. To his right.

"Really?"

He grunted, tracing the surface. Squinting at a subtle ripple. Even if nothing was out there, he should hurry them ashore. "Just another ten meters now."

She looked ahead. "Oh! I see it now. Thank you, Lord."

Something glimmered. Nerves tingling, Eamon urged the prop closer. "With as little movement as possible, slip off the prop and get to shore."

Ellis's eyes widened. Her gaze skimmed the waters as she silently, robotically moved. Surprisingly, she was more stealthy than he expected. He turned the prop, untying the material from his leg and stuffing it against the prop, which he then shoved in the opposite direction. It sputtered off and he stepped lightly through the water and made it to the shore.

Ellis started toward him. "Was it a croc?"

"Keep going," he said. "They aren't as fast on land, but fast enough." He guided them up the beach to where a trench harbored giant rocks and debris that had washed up there. From here, he had good line of sight on the yacht to make sure they weren't pursued, but it also kept them hidden so they could remain near shore for a rescue. "We can rest here."

Gripping his thigh, Eamon lowered himself to a rock with a grunt and leaned back against the cliff wall that rose another six meters. Roughing a hand over his head and face, Eamon glanced at his burning yacht.

She saw the jagged tear in his pants, shadowed by night, but she was pretty sure she also saw blood. "Is it bad?"

Eamon drew his leg up, away from her. "Just a scratch." He tore off a section of his shirt tail and when he did, she saw marred flesh on his arm. And a trail of blood on his shirt. "Eamon, your side!" She remembered the way he jerked just before the prop fell into the water. "You got shot?"

Grimacing as he tied the strip of shirt around his calf, he shook his head. "She'll be right." He strapped the cloth around his leg.

"What's that from?"

"A knife."

She gaped. "Stabbed, shot? Anything else?"

"Stranded," he said with a snort, angling to the side and dropping against the dirt wall, his gaze on the water. "Homeless."

That last word carried more pain than the other injuries, pushing Ellis's gaze out to his burning yacht. The sight knocked her back. "Oh Eamon," she whispered, slumping against the rock beside him, tears pricking her eyes. "I'm so sorry."

The yacht was groaning as its hull surrendered to the ferocious hunger of the fire. Creaks and pops carried across the distance to them with disheartening clarity. Ellis wished it was farther out, so he did not have to watch his ship go down.

Boom! A volley of fire shot into the air.

"Down she goes," he muttered, shouldering out of a pack. He opened it and dug around the wet contents. Pulled out a sealed pack and tore it open, using his teeth. "So much for the Beast of Cape York." He shifted to the side.

She shifted nearer, hurting for him. For what he'd been through. "Let me help." She nodded to the wound and his ministrations.

"Thought you weren't a good Scout?"

"That's when I was a child. I've grown a little since then."

"I'd say you have."

She eyed him, confused, but he handed her a pouch.

"Dry off the wound, then use the spray. Once it's clean, put two of those pills into the wound."

"Into it?" Ellis asked, her voice pitching. "It's dark—"

"Necessary. It'll stop the bleeding." He threaded his left arm out of the shirt and hooked his arm over his head and shifted to expose her side to him better.

Heaven's mercies. Ellis's mouth went dry at the sight of his very well-toned chest and abs—but his obliques! The Lord just didn't want her to have willpower, did He? "Right," she whispered. Digging out the spray and a clean sterile cloth, she adjusted her position to better let the moonlight aid her in cleaning the wound.

She dabbed the wound as gingerly as possible, but Eamon tensed, drew up and to the left. Away from the pain. Calming her nerves did no good knowing she was hurting him. But she continued, needing to be sure it was clean. Wasn't going to have him die of septic shock or something because she was a wimp with blood. When Eamon sucked in a breath and drew up straight, she knew she'd hurt him. Stomach knotted, she tensed. "Sorry."

"Doing good." His words were gritted, his hand fisted.

"Liar," she teased, enjoying the breath of a laugh that made his stomach contract. Done cleaning, she lifted the spray and aimed it at his side. Gave a quick squeeze.

"More," Eamon grunted. But he jerked when she obeyed. He tilted his head back and closed his eyes.

Heat washed over her. Coldness filled her belly. She wet her lips and refocused on the wound, whispering a prayer for God to help her push past this to help him. She sprayed and held it a little longer, sweeping it across the angry flesh.

"Good."

"Not really," she muttered, reaching for the pills, feeling sick to her stomach that she'd have to push them into the hole. She swallowed the metallic taste in her mouth as she looked to the wound again. Her stomach seemed ready to revolt. "Just . . . stick them in?"

Eamon gave a curt nod. "They'll expand. Stop me from bleeding out."

Right. Staying alive was good. "Both at the same time?"

"First one. If it doesn't go far, then we don't need the other."

Ellis climbed onto her knees. Not that it gave her a better angle, but this . . . this was about to make her spew her cookies. Darts of fire shot up her inner forearms as she reached toward the wound.

Blood glubbed out.

Her stomach churned. Ears rang.

Do it. Before you can't. She plunged one into the wound.

Eamon jerked. Grunted. Growled. Tucked his neck and arched his spine.

Oh God—help! That hurt him.

In revolt, her stomach roiled. Bile rose in her throat. *I'm going to be sick.*

"Ellis."

She was going to vomit. Was it getting darker? Had a cloud passed over the fingernail moon? *Do this. For him. Don't be weak.*

Hands framed her face. "Ellis."

Eyes snapped to his, she drew in her a breath. Struggled past the nausea and hollowing of her ears—and gasped. "You said my name!" Panic and relief warred.

"How did you know? I . . . I couldn't tell you. I can't tell anyone. Ever." Her ears felt weird. "They wouldn't let me. It was—"

"Shhh," he said, the ridge of his strong brow tensing. "Easy, easy." Soothing, his voice lulled her into a quiet. "Sit back."

"Your side—"

"I can finish it."

"No," Ellis said, snapping straight. Shook her head. Blinked. "I'm fine."

"You're not."

"You've done enough for me. I can do this for you." It took a few seconds for her head to clear, but she would not fail him. He had never let her down. It was her turn to repay the favor. Fingers gently braced around the wound, Ellis applied a swath of gauze and taped it on. "There." She slumped back, wiping the sweat from her brow. Holding the back of her hand to her mouth.

Through the exhaustion and tumult, she landed on one thought: he knows. It was freeing yet terrifying for someone to know the truth. No. That wasn't it. It was freeing and terrifying that *he* knew. "How did you know—about me?"

"My mum," he said, his gaze still on the burning hulk. "She said I couldn't let you die because you were Ellis." He coiled his fist again and his nostrils flared.

"Do you have painkillers?"

"Can't take them. Need my wits about me."

Though she told herself not to, Ellis slipped her hand over his. He went still. Very still. Deathly still. And it unnerved her, but since he hadn't thrown her off, she stayed. She didn't apologize again for the loss of his yacht or give idle words that would reiterate what he already knew. She just sat there in silence, letting him grieve. Not only did Eamon lose his yacht, he had been the one to blow it up. She could not imagine the agony roiling through the big warrior. Moonlight caught movement, and she saw his fingers, dangling over his drawn-up knee, coiling into a fist. Uncoiling. Coiling.

Persistent and fierce, he'd fought his way through the yacht. Protected the guests. Protected her. And at the pool, he'd knocked the guy in and held him there. For. Ever. Drowned him. Saved her. On the prop, he'd detected her trembling and leaned into her. It'd been glorious to have his reassuring warmth. She ached for it now, too. Time and again. And it cost him everything. So much like twenty years ago. Their families had been skiing in the Alps together. One night, the adults had gone out for the evening, leaving Eamon and Ellis alone. Kidnappers broke in and snatched them both. Truth of it was, they'd only wanted Ellis, but Eamon, his warrior spirit alive even then, refused to be left behind. Hidden in the smelly crawlspace of a shack for over a week, they'd finally escaped. A harrowing nightmare that nearly killed Ellis.

Realizing he'd gone silent, she glanced up to see if Eamon had fallen asleep. Of course, he hadn't. He stared in brooding silence at his ship. That strong profile, the hard edge of his jaw twitching the muscle there.

He was a beached Poseidon forced to watch his kingdom sink into the depths.

CHAPTER 14

GAME CHANGER. EVERYTHING changed, knowing Ellis was alive and sat beside him. That he hadn't been responsible for her death because she hadn't even died. All these years he'd spent forming his career and focus to be a protector, to save those who couldn't save themselves . . .

"You must hate me," Ellis whispered.

Against the cliff, Eamon rolled his head back and forth. "Nah. No energy for it."

"But your mum said you went into the SAS because of me. Well, not *me*, but because you believed I'd died."

He felt her gaze on him, those wide green eyes that had gone from childlike innocence and terror the last time he'd seen her to wide-eyed wonder and beauty now. Somehow, finding out she was Ellis had changed more than watching his boat sink. How, he wasn't sure. Maybe there was more at stake. Sensing she needed an affirmation that she hadn't messed up his life or that his career had been good—all because of a little girl who supposedly died—Eamon could answer honestly. "I have no regrets," he said finally and firmly. "And I wouldn't change any of what I did. It was important."

"Why?"

"Because it needed to be done." His internal life movie played across his vision. Swung him from the dead-of-night flight in the Alps to save Ellis twenty years ago, to the betrayal by Brie, to the mission that killed Cory Niehauer. "To fight evil. To protect the innocent—it needed to be done." He'd done good things, serving his country, protecting it from those who would do harm.

The specter of death wreathed the *ViCross*. Dropping shadows like spirits fleeing the burning hulk. Eamon tensed, Ellis and the pain blurring out of focus as he saw two distinct shapes spiriting across the water. Moving with intent. Not like chunks of rail and windows crashing into the sea. Red dots appeared.

Not spirits. Operators.

They're coming.

"I'm—"

Eamon punched to his feet and clenched through the blinding pain in his side as he caught Ellis's arm. "Go."

"Wha—"

"Run!" He thrust her down the beach.

Sand fought their momentum, slowing them. Wrestling them with each step. Struggling against their escape. No worse than carrying weights in the pool, but the bullet in his side was screaming against the jostling. It could do some serious damage to his ability to negotiate this situation. Maybe cause serious damage to his ability to survive at all.

Darkness yawned to the left where a section of the cliff carved away from the water.

"Here, here," Eamon hissed, catching her shirt and tugging her back. Slapping a hand on his side as the pain roared. When Ellis slipped, he wanted to curse. But she found her footing and came round. He shoved her on, glancing at the quickly approaching red lights coming for them.

The jagged well, formed by cliffs on either side, was stuffed with rocks and debris that had washed up on shore. Ellis climbed the rocky terrain, her movements fast, but not fast enough.

Irritation and pain pinched his focus. Invited him to compromise their safety.

Eamon pushed himself, as he always had. Yet his mind

screamed that this route was not good. That instead of saving them, he was driving them straight into death's arms. That though he'd saved her twenty years ago, tonight he'd get her killed.

Ellis clawed at the dirt wall to clear the last half-dozen feet. But she lost traction. Slid. Right back into him. Took out his right leg. Spiked pain through his side. He lost his focus. Dropped on her. With a growl, Eamon struggled to catch himself and not crush her against the rocks. When he landed on her, she yelped and tensed.

He slid his hand along her waist, bracing her. Bracing them both. "You okay?"

Though she nodded, he noted she wasn't talking and told himself to slow down, give her time to find a good pace. But the drone of props grew closer, louder. She was going to get them killed.

Eamon chided himself for that thought. "C'mon," he said, quieter, softer. Not as forceful. He kept his hand on her waist, telling himself it was to help her. To encourage her to keep moving not give up. But her curve gave him the painful reminder that she was not in a tactical vest. That she was not one of his mates. That she was a woman.

No. She was Ellis. Family friend. Nine years younger. He'd saved her once. Could he do it again?

Like a spider, Ellis took to the cliff again, resolute on reaching the top, conquering the terrain. Finally, she hooked a leg over the wall and hoisted herself atop the cliff. Shifted back and he vaulted himself over and came up. Weakness and pain flooded him. His knee buckled.

"Eamon!"

"Fine," he gritted out, holding out a staying hand.

Which she slipped hers into and clasped tight. He stared at her fingers dwarfed in his. Felt a betraying rush of thrill. Annoyed at himself, he led her from the edge. They were like figures in a shooting gallery up here. He scanned, his gut cinching tight. The trees were dense. Easy to get lost. Lose their bearing. Filled with—

Crack!

Ellis cried out and tripped.

Pulse roaring, Eamon lunged at her. Took her to the ground, covering her body with his. Arm shielding her head, he breathed against her ear, "Stay down." Peering ahead through the darkness to the trees, he sought the quickest route. What he wouldn't give to use his night-vision goggles, but they were too close. Too easily spotted.

Even as he plotted the route, he shifted his mind to her. "Where'd you get hit?"

"Shoulder," she said around a grimace. "Right side."

He eased back, lifting his chest, and checked. Her blouse was torn, pale flesh glaring with blood. Swept his thumb along it. She hissed, but the feel of the wound was more consistent with a lesser injury. "I think it's a graze," he shifted off her, arm around her again. "See the trees?"

Ellis lifted her head, squinting. "I think so."

"Think you can make it?"

She nodded.

"Ready?"

Another nod and her arms were winging out to push herself up.

"Zigzag. Go." Eamon rose behind her, deliberately stepping behind her to block anymore incoming fire. The graze didn't slow her. The girl had some pretty serious speed on her.

Eamon paced her, cringing each time he heard the report of the weapon. Knew that the speed of sound closely paralleled the speed of a bullet. He'd hear it and feel it nearly at the same time from this distance. Felt the sting of rocks and dirt spit at them.

With a leap, Ellis plunged into the trees and immediately slowed. But with the way the limbs thwatted and slapped at them, Eamon knew the shooters must have the advantage of NVGs and a sniper scope, so he let his momentum carry him past her. "Farther," he said, pulling her into the thick darkness of the trees.

Navigating the blackness proved treacherous because they couldn't see the floor, couldn't see traps, or animals lurking among the trunks and branches. He had night-vision goggles, but using them risked exposure because of the telltale flare of green. Creatures or bullets. One threat or another existed. Prevented them from stopping. And yet his tactical brain told him each step separated them from safety. Made his own injury worse.

I will not let her die this time either.

Almost at once, he felt the absence of her presence. "Ellis?"

"Here," she said, her voice sodden with fear and fright.

He reached and their hands tangled, then he caught her and pulled her close. Placed her hand on the drag strap of his vest. "Hold on. Okay?"

"Yeah," she said. She sounded as worn out and annoyed as he did.

Eamon trudged ahead, reaching back to his ruck thinking to use his NVGs once they got deeper in. They'd get in a bit farther then take a break. Watch the edge of the trees for their pursuers. Goggles in hand, he resisted the temptation for as long as he could, not wanting to give them away.

A hard pull on the drag strap yanked him backward. Then . . . nothing. "Ell—"

Grunts and yelps fell away in a chaos of crushed branches, sliding rocks and dirt and came to a thudding finality with a thick *oof*. The sound of a body impacting something solid.

Eamon whipped toward the noise. "Ellis!" Dead of night and the dark scrub forbid him from seeing ahead. He snapped up the goggles, scanning but saw nothing but the black veil. "Ellis!"

"Down here." Her voice was small but still close.

Meager and stingy, the moon granted a stray beam of light through swaying braches that sorted the shadows and shapes. He had narrowly missed the crevasse that Ellis had discovered. At least six or seven meters deep, it had swallowed her.

"Watch that step," she said. "It's a doozie."

A smile tugged him closer. He detected the bush floor dipping away. Slid-skidded down the embankment. Felt her hand against his calf. To the side. He lowered himself to a crouch and listened for her. "Hurt?"

"No," she said. "Just . . . fed up. Tired."

Wind rustled the air, branches whispering secrets and threats. Unless the shooters followed their path directly, this crevasse should be as good as any place to hunker down. They both needed a respite.

She struggled to her feet.

"Here," he said, catching her hand and drawing her to the side, beneath a small overhang. It also shielded them from a direct line of sight from the north. "Sit. Rest."

"Thank God," she whispered and collapsed in the ravine.

Holding his side, Eamon lowered himself to the ground beside her. Legs up, wrists propped on his knees, he tilted his head back and stared up at the opening, anticipating trouble. It'd come. Eventually. Always did.

Their shoulders touched marginally, bungeeing his attention back to her more than he'd care to admit. She wasn't an alpha female, but she was tough. Strong and intelligent. Incredible all that she'd pulled off with the complex, a dream he wasn't sure would ever be realized. She'd said her heart was attached to the business proposal. To the complex. Which meant it was important to her.

He snorted. His first clue that he'd been dealing with a female and not the fake Vic Toriael should've been the lengthy emails. They were wordy—speaking to the heart of the complex, to helping diggers who'd come back from the war, and their families and those relationships. Women typically found that a priority. To him, he wanted to help a buddy in trouble. One of his own.

"Eamon."

"Yeh?" he said quietly.

"Do you remember that night?"

He didn't need to ask which one. It'd been seared into his memory. "Yep."

"Saving me twice in as many decades."

"Let's not go for a third," he muttered.

She laughed softly—apparently as concerned over giving away their location as he was. "Agreed." After a sigh, she shifted, leaning against him a little more. "I'm sorry they lied to you, and to everyone else about me."

It made sense, he guessed. "It was necessary." Only as he thought that did Eamon register the truth of it—she was royalty. That made him snort again.

"It was, but . . . it still caused pain."

"Agreed," he said lightly, and when she laughed his mind split in two. The first finding pleasure that he made her laugh, not as boisterous as she had on the ViCross, but still. And the second mind: that blasted annoyance that she was here, that he was responsible for her. That he had to protect her again from dying.

No, that wasn't why he was annoyed. He did that for a living. Why would it bother him now?

Warmth. Her breath. The sun deck. Her attraction. His attraction.

No. He wasn't attracted to Ellis. She was nine years his junior. Young. Innocent. Beautiful. Willing.

No. No, he wasn't going to do that.

Never again. *Remember, idiot?*

CHAPTER 15

ELLIS HATED THAT not only could she not see his eyes, she couldn't even see his face. He'd grown more and more annoyed with her since they'd hit the beach and she wasn't sure why.

Because he knows who you are now.
What difference did that make?

Was it because her identity had been hidden? That everyone, including his mum, had lied to him? Tension tightened his bicep pressing against her shoulder. The threat of hating her hung between them as the minutes fell away. She tried to keep her eyes open, to not be a simpering woman with no tactical experience. More than that, she wanted every morsel of deceit between them gone. Desperation clung to her to rid their relationship—if one could call it that—of all these roadblocks and frustrations. But that was a dream.

Her eyelids grew heavy. Her mind heavier.

Through a thick haze, she heard a sound. Muffled. Warbling. She shifted.

Felt something clamp over her mouth.

Ellis jerked up, only then realizing Eamon's hand covered her mouth. She'd fallen asleep—on his shoulder. She slowly lifted her head and his hand fell away, only to return, this time with a weapon. His gaze remained focused on the top of the ravine where shadows drifted past them.

Voices skated through a light fog. And only then did Ellis's mind register the amount of light. She must've slept a couple of hours. And it'd taken these men that long to find them.

"Thermals must be buggy," one of the men said.

"Couple of big cats, maybe," another said. "Do they have cats here?"

"Negative," the other responded. "Wallabies and dingoes, but the real threats won't show up on thermals."

"Sounds a lot like it's time to head back, then."

"He won't like that."

"Yeah, and I don't like mucking around some forest in search of a man he couldn't kill on the yacht. Not my problem," the man said as he trudged past the ravine. "If he wants us to come back, he'll have to wait until daylight."

"Or never," the other guy laughed, giving a scant look down at them.

Right at them!

Expecting to be discovered, Ellis held her breath, afraid they'd hear the frantic knocking of her heart.

Eamon's hand closed around hers and he squeezed, the movement so subtle, so stealthy, she froze.

Only as the man kept moving did she notice the brush that covered them. Branches. Leaves. Eamon must've camouflaged them while she slept. As the voices grew more distant, Eamon shifted. "To your left. Go. Follow the ravine."

Truth be told, she wasn't sure she could move let alone run but as quietly as she could, she pushed to her feet and clambered away from their hiding spot. The last few hours had been the most exhausting of her life!

A strange glow from above seemed to direct them down the narrow sliver of space. Ellis trailed her hands on either side more to be sure she walked a straight line than anything else. The steady cadence of Eamon's firm pace pushed her onward.

It'd been her dream. More like a fantasy. That she would be reunited with Eamon. She might have only been six when he saved her, but the memory of him as a teenager being all heroic was as real and present as his breath on her neck even now. "Do you remem—"

"Quiet."

Biting her tongue at the retort that sprang up from the hurt of his clipped tone, Ellis complied. Because it was for the better. Yet there was more to his tone. Irritation. But he had reason, she told herself. She, this person thrown into his life and depending on his protection, was a liability. Isn't that what Thor said? And not only that, but she'd lied to him.

Alaina had told her about Lieutenant Hastings. How she'd lied and seduced Eamon to get her way, to pass intel to the enemy. He hadn't dated since then. It'd also been his mum who'd shown her the scrapbook when she was fifteen—the same age Eamon had been when he'd saved her life. The handsome young man in the clippings kept his head high but there was a ferocity behind those blue eyes that she hadn't remembered from Courchevel. He'd been funny. Told her jokes. She hadn't known it then as a kid, but he'd probably been distracting her.

Where was that person? The one who'd so carefully protected both the mind and body of a six year old? The man stalking her pushed.

But he did . . . he did protect her still. Not just physically. He'd kept things from her so she didn't worry. The croc. He'd detected it in the water. Tariq—he hadn't told her that Tariq died.

Her legs were aching, but she kept moving, refusing to give him a reason to snap at her again. She'd made him angry once; she didn't want to do it again. There was something feral about his anger that made her sick to her stomach. Made her feel like she'd failed.

A grunt came from behind.

Ellis glanced over her shoulder. He wasn't there. The realization stopped her short, heart ramming into her throat. "Ea—"

"Keep going," he said, his words thick as he emerged from

the darkness.

She stumbled around, planting one foot in front of the other. Uncertainty dogged her steps as she traced the ravine that curved through the dense foliage, then rose, lifting them back to the bush floor and exposing them. She couldn't help but quicken her steps, however, she also noticed Eamon was slowing. Why had he fallen behind earlier? Why was his face mottled with sweat? It was hot, but not *that* hot. Then again, she wasn't carrying a ruck.

Or a bullet.

Worry creased her thoughts, folding them in on her, letting her see for the first time that Poseidon might be mortal after all. She'd never imagined that he wouldn't get her out alive. But her legs were aching. More like numb. She wasn't sure she could feel them. And she wasn't wearing hiking boots, so the blisters forming in her shoes were searing. She stumbled a bit, yearning for a rest. Though she had no idea how long they'd walked, she guessed at least an hour. Couldn't they rest? "Think we lost them?" she braved.

"Maybe." The word was more like a grunt.

"When can we—"

Behind her, he stumbled. Bumped into her. *Oof.*

Alarm twisted her around. Surprise punched her—he was on a knee. Head down. Shoulders rising and falling. Ellis went to him and touched his back. "Eamon?"

"Fine, I'm fine," he muttered, staggering to his feet.

"You are not. I think we should rest—you need the rest."

"I *need* to get you to safety," he bit out.

"You can't do that dead, and that's exactly where you're driving yourself."

He hesitated, hovering over her, looking back the way they'd come, then in the direction they were headed.

INDECISION HELD HIM fast. Behind them the enemy were coming. He could hear them, see the blips of their NVGs bleeding through the darkness every now and then. Ahead, they would only find an outback-like terrain and no protection from the sun. Behind them only thick trees and tangoes. Death on both sides. Little hope.

If they ventured onward, they also put themselves farther from the rendezvous point he'd given Thor. With their pursuers coming, they couldn't go back. But the scrub—a stretch of isolated land with no hope of a passing car or tourist—meant heat, no protection from the sun, ravenous creatures, snakes, and little chance of help.

Eamon closed his eyes and lowered his head, shaking it in defeat.

"Only a few minutes," Ellis said, her hands resting on his forearms. "Until we catch our breath."

He couldn't concede the point because it felt too much like conceding their lives. And control. "Just a little further." And he turned and forced his boots to move forward, one in front of the other. One step at a time.

"This is so much like Courchevel," Ellis said softly. "Just when I'd thought I couldn't go on anymore, you always pushed me farther."

"And I got you shot."

"*And* now, I've returned the favor," she said, motioning to his side. "Does this make us even?"

"This wasn't about you," Eamon ground out, his words an effort, the march more so. "He came after me."

"I heard, but you can't blame yourself—"

"I can," he growled. "I do. If I hadn't let Brie—" Eamon chomped off the words. "I made a mistake—"

"You fell in love with a spy."

He shouldn't be surprised. "Anything my mum didn't tell you?"

"Your shoe size."

He smirked. Snorted a laugh, then shook his head. "She got in my head," Eamon said as he took a slower pace. "Made me doubt myself. Next op, my team was out-positioned and outgunned. We had one mission: target and neutralize a senior Taliban commander in the war against Coalition forces." Strange that he was telling her since he hadn't spoken of it since he'd given his testimony. Not since he had to bury Niehauer and visit the others in hospital. "I got key intel from a female interpreter. I noticed something. Saw it in her eyes. Didn't think I could trust her. But I was so worried about letting Brie get in my head and stay there, that I shrugged it off. Gave the intel to the team. We went in, couple of Black Hawks, Apache gunships to ferry in the blokes." He shook his head, sighting a copse of trees with thick trunks. Maybe that would work. "We're fifty meters from the structure when a machine gun opens up on us. We had to crawl because we couldn't get up."

"That's when you got the scars?"

"Went in, dragging them out, dragging out Niehauer while under heavy fire."

"That put you in danger though," she said, as if she couldn't understand why he took the risk.

"Better to face that fire than the families of my mates who might die."

"Like Niehauer."

He sniffed. "Extreme response to my failure."

"Failure? But you won—the news declared it. I read the articles—airstrikes took out the location as you were clearing the hill, the Taliban there were killed."

Eamon stopped, looked at her shadowed face. "Killing isn't winning." He huffed, a hand planted on his side, which felt more damp than it should. The bandage must be leaking. "Winning is achieving your objective without loss of life. You lose one guy, then you've lost."

And he'd failed Cory Niehauer. Failed himself. Another

reason he couldn't fail this mission. The tangled beauty of a strangler fig tree loomed nearby. Thick vines coiled around the tree trunk and would eventually strangle the tree itself. He motioned to it. "Here." He shouldered out of the pack. "We'll take twenty."

Ellis moved to sit down.

"No," he said. "Up there." He pointed to the thick limbs of the trees that threaded together, forming a kind of bench between the two trunks. "They won't be looking up."

"We hope," she said softly and started to climb.

Perched on the tangle of branches, Eamon leaned back against the thick trunk. Dragged off the ruck and breathed a little easier. Only then did he realize the exhaustion plying at his limbs and mind. On his watch, he set the timer to vibrate in twenty minutes. Arms folded, he tucked his chin to his chest and closed his eyes.

She was there. In the shadows of his haunted past and just six years old with long, strawberry blond hair. Green eyes. Why hadn't he noticed the resemblance before now? Even then, she'd trusted him despite being traumatized and scared.

Just like now.

He wasn't sure how he'd earned that respect before or even now. He'd treated her poorly on the *ViCross*. Been rough with her now.

Why? It wasn't her fault.

Did it matter? He was keeping her alive. That didn't require manners.

But he had an inner moral code that wouldn't allow him to bring himself down out of spite. Because of Brie. Because of the mistake he'd made there. Falling for her. Loving her— God help him, he'd loved Brie Hastings.

"What was she like?"

Eamon twitched, realizing he was half asleep with her on his mind. He roughed a hand over his face. "What? Who?"

"Brie."

He huffed. "Rest, Ellis."

"I can't sleep," she argued.

"I didn't say sleep. I said rest," he snapped. "Your body needs it. I need it. Remember?"

"Understood," she said, her voice cracked with the hurt he'd just inflicted. And he didn't care.

Yes, he did. He did care. Too much. Too much for their wellbeing.

Crack!

Eamon froze at the sound that came from straight ahead. And close. His heart rapid-fired, watching gunmen bleed into a perimeter around them. Six. All around them. He caught Ellis's arm and tugged her against him. Pressed his mouth to her ear. "Don't move," he breathed as he lifted his weapon from the thigh holster.

Their luck was running out. So was the scrub. About another dozen paces, he could see the hostile terrain. Little cover to protect them from bullets or the scorching sun that was already climbing up into its seat of power. That wasn't the worst of his worries. The fever in his side told him that even if Ellis made it out of this alive, he probably wouldn't. The bullet was aggravating the wound, his internal organs. He'd go septic if they had to leave this nest above the forest.

CHAPTER 16

ELLIS HAD NEVER prayed so hard in her life as she did that moment, watching the half-dozen armed men drift around the forest floor beneath them. She'd thought they had gotten a reprieve when they climbed up into the tree, but now she felt vulnerable with air bubbling around them. What would they do if one of the men looked up, somehow saw past the limbs and shadows to what was hidden in the tree?

A shout in the distance felt like a bat striking Ellis's chest. She sucked in a breath and froze.

The men below did the same. One lifted a hand and made a signal. "This way," he called.

"What's he want? We had a sighting," one of the men grumbled.

"It's his problem," another said. "We found blood, so they're not going to get far."

"He's got more men," a gravelly voice reported. "Maybe we can get this over with and get out of this godforsaken place."

More men? Ellis didn't dare look at Eamon, but the thought of more guns pointed at her made her heart race.

"Move. Now," Eamon breathed again, the heat of his mouth and words sending a tremor down her spine. He was swinging down out of the trees with little effort.

She scrambled after him, hesitating when she saw him hit the ground. A leg buckled and with a labored effort he rose again. Ellis hooked the limbs and slid over the side, dangling.

"Release," he hissed.

Ellis did, and halfway down, his hands clamped onto her waist. Eased her descent. A rock beneath her foot pitched her into his chest, and he angled her around. Caught her hand—not for any romantic notion, she realized, but so he didn't have to speak and give them away.

They jogged in the opposite direction of the men, the lightening sky laying plain before them the barren land. Her heart dropped as they rushed forward, realizing they were in the open. Nowhere to hide. No way to conceal where they were. If Niehauer's men caught up, it'd be easy pickings.

Eamon knew it, too, of course. In a crouch, he aimed them around shrubs and small mounds, anything to conceal them. But it was like trying to hide a truck behind a telephone pole.

"How are we going to do this?" she wondered out loud as the isolated terrain yawned wide before them and went on . . . and on . . . in the far distance rugged clefts shot up defiantly. Even now with the sun still struggling from it slumber and pushing back the blue-black of the sky, she felt the difference in the air. Within the shade of the forest, it'd been lush. Easy to breathe, though still quite warm. Arid and dry, this land offered nothing but a chance to go a little crazy with panic and eventually, hallucinations from dehydration.

Water. "I'm thirsty."

Eamon huffed and freed a tube from the shoulder strap of his pack. "Here. Drink slowly and only a little. It's nearly done for."

Surprised, Ellis stepped over to him, feeling awkward that she had to stand so close to take a draught from the CamelBak. She took the bite valve and had to tiptoe up to reach. The awkward pose made her unsteady. She swayed forward and his arm slid around her waist and held her. His chin and gaze angled to her.

Careful not to spit on him when she released the valve, she managed a sheepish grin as she eased back down.

"Better?" He took a draught then secured the valve.

Not really, but she wasn't going to complain. "I'll live."

"I'm counting on that." With his other hand, he reached back and shouldered out of the pack, eyes scrunching as he did. Walking again, Eamon dug into a pocket and retrieved two protein bars. He handed her one, tucked one in his pocket, then geared back up. The bar helped her stamina, but not her exhaustion. There wasn't anything that would help that but to sleep for a week.

As they hiked, their exhaustion rose with the morning sun, which spread its glory over the Northern Territory, brightening the already-vibrant swath of red that cut through the scrub. The isolation and unforgiving terrain with its red sand, scraggly trees and bushes, then the obstinate boulder that jutted out of nowhere proved daunting. So incongruent. One expected more browns, but the arid region apparently had its own rules. And natural wildlife.

"Oi," he said quietly, shifting toward her and angling a shoulder in. He pointed in the distance. "A boomer."

Kangaroo? Really? She pushed on her tiptoes and craned her neck to see, but she only saw more red and green. Red and green. "Where?"

Eamon shifted behind her and his face lowered next to hers. His arm came from the other side. "There," he said.

Stomach swirling at his presence, Ellis did her best to stifle the way her body betrayed her at his presence. Roos. He was showing her kangaroos. She blinked. Refocused on the ter—"There!" Kangaroos bounded across a long, red swath of the brutal land. Then more. "Joeys! Wow, I've never seen so many."

"A whole mob," Eamon said, smiling at her. His gaze swept over her and she felt the thrill of his attention. He drew out a cap and a scarf. After setting the cap on his own head, he lifted the scarf over hers. Wrapped it around her face. The relief was immediate and wonderful.

"At least we can keep your head from getting scorched," he said as he looped it around her neck.

Did he realize how close he was? Hovering over her with a mere two inches between them, between their lips. His stubbled jaw. The way the left side of his face where the scar was pulled up toward the eye with that perpetual smirk, pinching his beautiful blue eyes and accenting the lines at the corners of his eyes, carved by his time in the sun during his commando years. His presence was powerful. When he was in front of her, the world fell away. He was so beautiful, in a rugged, hewn from granite sort of way. She'd never noticed that he had thin lips that made his jaw seem that much more angular. Sweat and dirt mottled his brow and that strong ridge over his eyes that seemed more knotted than usual, pushing her gaze to his.

But he wasn't looking at her. He was looking at her lips.

Her stomach squirmed, breath stalling in her throat as he angled closer.

Her mind straddling the awe of seeing the roos and the possibility of Eamon's kiss, her brain squeezed out some words. "Don't see roos from the *ViCross*, I bet," she murmured, anxious in anticipation. The one he'd withdrawn on the sundeck when everything went wrong between them.

And with those words, it went wrong again. She saw it.

The granite returning to cold steel. The dropped gaze. The step back. "Won't see anything on the *ViC* anymore." His expression went grim, taking the lighthearted moment with it.

"I'm sorry, Eamon."

"Sorry doesn't bring my boat back." Head down, shoulders sagging, he trudged forward. His foot dragged. He shuffled. Caught himself. He shook his head and pushed on.

Hurt, annoyed that he'd yet again withdrawn from her, Ellis stumbled after him. "Are you mad at me, Eamon?"

Walking but not talking. His gait seemed uneven. But it was hot at blazes out here and they had no hope of help or rescue in sight. The sun high above beat them with unrelenting strength. Searing their skin.

"Just tell me," Ellis said, skipping a step to catch up. "How do I make this barrier between us go away? Tell me, and I'll do it."

"You can't."

She scoffed. "Why? What is it? Is it Brie? Are you punishing me because of her?"

"You lied to me, Ellis."

"And I apologized for it."

The terrain rolled upward, forcing them to work harder in the unrelenting heat. Her head throbbed. "Why do you do this, Eamon? It's a pattern, you know that, right?"

He kept walking.

"You went into the army. Left your parents. You were a phenomenal commando. But you got out. Then hid on the *ViCross*."

"Which is destroyed, thanks to you."

"To me?" she pitched. When he again ignored her words, she raced around him, noticing and thanking God for the relief of another scraggly tree. "Me? That man didn't want me dead, remember? You told me he came after *you*!"

"And your deceptive event created the conditions in which he could get onto my boat."

She wanted to shove him. Which would be like slapping a boulder. But then it dawned on her. "No."

Squinting beneath that ball cap, he cocked his head. "Come again?"

"No, this isn't about me and that event. It's about you," she argued. "You need to forgive yourself—"

He snorted. Tried to brush past her, but Ellis pushed back with a hefty grunt.

"No. You're not walking away from this or me anymore. What is wrong with you? Are you afraid you might actually like me?"

His jaw tightened.

"What's so bad with giving me a chance?"

"I have one goal: get you home alive." His eyes bored into her. "*Again*, apparently. And after this, I won't see you. I won't—" He snapped his mouth shut.

Ellis frowned at the words he'd retracted. "You won't what?"

"Leave it, Ellis."

She growled in frustration. "No." She shrugged, surprised at herself for being so oppositional—had to be the heat—but she was so fed up with his reticence. "I see the way you look at me." When he closed in on her, she was forced back a step. "That's twice now you've nearly kissed me. But you walk away. During the social, you couldn't keep your eyes off me. And don't you dare tell me it was because you thought I was a threat. You're a freakin' commando. If you can't sort a threat from attraction—"

"It's better this way." He edged closer.

"Why?" Ellis shifted to give herself room. "Because there's no risk? Because you can't guarantee the outcome?"

"Yes!" he barked.

"So, you're a coward."

His eyes blazed.

And her heart hiccupped. "I . . . I didn't mean that. I'm just—" She stumbled over a root and looked to make sure she had space—

His chest wall pinned her against the tree. His mouth was on hers. The kiss was hard and angry, but as she melted into his arms, it grew hungry, demanding. Crushed between him and the tree, Ellis slid her hands up his arms and shoulders.

He cupped her face, deepening the kiss with a moan that awakened her own longing. But then he stilled, veered off. Moved his head to the side. He was sagging . . . like an ice sculpture melting beneath the cruelty of the heat.

"Eamon?" This time, she cupped his face. Gasped—his

face was clammy. Feverish. "Eamon, talk to me."

Eyes closed, he slumped against the tree. "I just..." His lids flicked open. Eyes widened. He swallowed.

Ellis released the bite valve and pushed it to his mouth. "Eamon, drink."

He started to object.

"Do it," she snapped, panic marching through her chest.

His blue eyes struck hers. Pinched with a pained smile. He wet his own cracked lips and accepted the valve. Took a draught.

"More," she insisted.

"It's gone," he said hoarsely.

Ellis looked at the valve, mind racing. Heart racing. Lost out here with no water?

Hunching his shoulders, Eamon held his side and groaned. His nostrils flared beneath an apparent wave of pain. Face reddening, he grabbed onto the tree. Held himself up.

"We need to rest. Sit down—"

"No. Too many dangers."

"But you need rest."

Eamon huffed. "We keep walking."

"You mean stumbling!"

"Whatever gets us there."

"Where?"

Heavy-lidded eyes looked past her. His brow rose.

Ellis peered over her shoulder and only saw more of the same bush-like land, the striking stretch of red sand, and a cliff in the distance.

"High ground," he said.

She swung around. "Eamon, that's at least ten kilometers!"

"Then we"—he gritted through a breath—"better get going."

A NOISE LURED him from a weighted sleep. Something was wrong. Claxons screeched through his mind as he struggled to the surface. Blackness crowded his vision. He groaned, fighting his way back from whatever held him down. Panic beat against his ribs, sending thuds of pain through his side, all the way up to his head. Something was wrong. Very wrong. *Where am I?*

"Eamon, Eamon. It's me. It's okay. Quiet." The voice was soft, plaintive. Familiar. Threw images across his mind, a heated one of a killer kiss.

He slumped in defeat. "Ellis? Why can't I see?"

She sniffed. "Because we're in a cave. And it's dark out."

Dark? Eamon jerked upright. Shards of fire scored his side. He howled and dropped back.

"Just be still, Eamon. You're very sick."

"How—" The word caught in his throat. He forced a swallow but it did no good. His tongue was swelling. And it was so blasted hot. "How long . . . ?"

"I . . . I'm not sure," Ellis said, sounding small and frightened. "Hours. I've tried to find water, but . . ."

Hearing the pain and panic in her voice undid something in him. "It's okay." He reached toward where he'd heard her voice. Touched skin. Her hands caught his. But a frightening truth struck him: "I don't remember getting here." Something cool touched his forehead, opening his eyes. Her hand drew away, but he ached for the cool touch once more.

"I'm not surprised. You were half out of it for the last kilometer or two."

I'm failing her. "I can't . . . remember."

"Well, you collapsed. Then I had to drag you up here."

"*You* dragged me?"

"Yeah, I'd say you should lose some weight, but I think I like you as you are."

Smiling at the teasing in her voice, he managed, "Beast of Cape York?"

"I don't think he exists," she whispered.

Her fingers traced the scar on his face and Eamon let his eyes close. His thoughts fell back to what he did remember—that kiss. He'd lost it when she'd railed at him. Lost it because she'd called him on his attitude. Called him on his rail-thin excuses and nailed the truth on the head. The truth he hadn't been able to see. Hadn't let himself see. He was afraid of what he felt for her.

She'd been six years old when he saw her last, so it wasn't like he had leftover attraction to explain the insanity prickling through his veins. Something about Ellis called to him. Anchored him.

He'd nearly jerked back when he'd plowed into that kiss, determined to show her what being kissed by him was like. That what she wanted wasn't what she'd get with him. That her conjured ideas of him were far from the truth.

But then she curled into him. Responded. Man, had she responded. And all the dead pieces of him reconstituted into something he'd never experienced before. Couldn't get enough of.

He shouldn't. Shouldn't give in to those yearnings. They'd gotten him into trouble with Brie. Got him focused on pleasure and not sense.

She's not Brie. He'd vowed the last two years that he'd never again put himself in that place. So why was he contemplating it with Ellis?

And it might not matter—this wound would probably kill him before they got rescued.

"Eamon," she called him back from the thoughts and darkness, "tell me what to do." A soft repetitive noise vied for his attention. "Tell me how to get help. I'm not a good Scout, remember?"

"You're better than you think," he muttered.

Hot breaths panted against his cheek. What the devil . . . ?

"Think we'll be rescued? I mean, we have to, right? How

else will we get out of here alive?"

Rescue! "My pack," he said. "Back, left pocket. There's an emergency beacon."

Ellis gasped. "Why didn't you use it before now?"

"Because it would draw everyone in a twenty-klick radius, including Niehauer."

"Okay, so why would we use it now, then? Won't he pick it up, too?"

"Need outweighs the risk," he grunted, unwilling to say he was dying.

"Right," she said. "Okay, I have it."

Eamon pried open an eye and the scant light from the cave opening caressed her face. Resilience and strength shone through the dehydration and exhaustion, the dirty face and loose strands of hair. "Take it. Walk a half-klick out, activate it, then bury it and return."

"What? Why not just activate it here? I don't want to leave you. Why so far away?"

"Because—the enemy will come just as easily. This way, we see who responds, can control betraying our location." Though a half-klick wouldn't give her much of a head start, at least she'd have that. Mind warring with the realization that he had no way to get her out of here, save setting off that beacon, which would probably bring Niehauer . . . who'd kill her.

Unless Thor answered the beacon first.

Eamon had broken plan. He was supposed to stay on the beach. Though he had a reasonable guess as to their location, he knew they were too far from the rendezvous point. But they'd be looking. Had to be.

Stay awake, Straider. She needs you.

The truth of it was, he needed her. Wanted her to fill that void. It was a perfect Ellis Rostov-Leclair-sized hole in his life that'd been ripped open when she'd "died" twenty years ago. And she'd returned. With laughter. Beauty. Belief.

With a sigh, he relaxed. Yeah . . . He'd been so convinced on the boat that something was off about her. And there was: She wasn't like anyone else he'd met and that guileless way of hers had reeled him in. Though she'd had the chance to save her own skin and leave on the speed boat, she'd gone back for him.

If she hadn't, she would've been safe.

She belongs with me.

Which was insane because she was going to be without him, thanks to this bullet making him septic. But what . . . what if he didn't die? He sure wasn't moving back to the city. And she was royalty, so she had to be around people. He didn't do people.

Maybe . . . maybe he could suffer humanity as long as he could retreat to his boat.

Which was at the bottom of the sea.

What was he thinking anyway? This was going way deeper than delirium. He was thinking about marriage. Sucking in a breath made him cough. Strained the wound. He growled and grabbed his side, arching his back at the same time.

"Eamon!" Ellis scurried back to his side and dropped beside him. "What happened?"

"I'll be okay."

That panting noise drifted on the air again and he squinted into the darkness to find the source.

"You have pills in the pack. Think you can choke them down?"

Indecision gripped his as he lay there, her thigh pressed against his ribs on the uninjured side. He rested a hand on her leg and worked to think through . . . He liked her close. Wanted her to stay close.

What was he thinking through?

"Just one?" Ellis pleaded.

He grunted—right. The pill.

Felt fingers at his lips. "Please—take it. You need it. We

can't do anything anyway."

"Have to move . . . closer . . . entrance," he managed.

"After you take the pill."

"One condition. You set the beacon first."

She sighed. "You're a tough negotiator. Okay." She shifted, the space around him chilling as she moved. "I'll be right back."

Eamon watched as her shape shrunk as she got farther away, then ducked through the opening and vanished. God, don't let anything happen to her. Antsy as the time fell off the clock without her return, he scooted toward the opening, but it felt like someone drove a telephone pole through his side. Growling he slumped against the cave wall again.

A sound outside made him freeze. He watched and strained to hear—crunching. Rocks slipping. Shoes. Then she was back.

Eamon breathed a sigh of relief, surprised at how much it'd bothered him that she was out there, exposed, and he couldn't protect her.

No. It was more than that. It wasn't just protection. He didn't want to lose her.

Insane.

"Okay," she mumbled as she crouched toward him, then went to her knees the last few feet. "Now your turn—the pill. Open up."

Eamon huffed. Ignored the humiliation of being hand-fed a pill and parted his lips.

She slipped it in. "Thank you."

He worked around the dry, swelling of his tongue to force down the capsule. But there wasn't enough saliva to carry it, so it stuck in his throat. Coughed. It came up and he just tucked it under his tongue, hating its bitterness.

"Why did you kiss me earlier?"

Eamon grunted, peeling himself off the floor of the cave. "We kissed?"

"You . . . you forgot that?"

He snorted. "How could I forget the way you pinned me?"

"Me? It was you!"

Eamon laughed, pain scoring the mistake of that teasing.

"Oh," she said softly, "you are cruel."

"So, I'm told," he chuckled as he sat up, trying to clear his head. "You know, you can't get a divorce for cruelty." He had no idea why he said that. Except that he did know. He was considering something he'd vowed to *never again* consider.

She stilled. "Um, to get a divorce, you have to be married first."

"Is that how it works?" Eamon breathed through the fiery darts running the gauntlet in his side.

"Should you be sitting up?"

"Have to get to the entran—" A wave of agony hit him. He lowered his head and rolled his neck, gritting through it. His gaze struck the light a dozen meters away. "The entrance."

Ellis helped him make their way back to the front.

"How'd you find this cave?" he asked, as they got closer and he saw it wasn't at eye level.

Something furry brushed against his arm. Thinking it a spider, he flicked it away.

"I saw a dog come out."

A high-pitched keening noise pierced the relative quiet of the cave. Eamon twitched, staring down at the little pup.

"Oh, how sweet," Ellis said, her voice amused. "He's kept me company."

Eamon's heart rapid-fired when he saw the four-legged animal, the moonlight reaching into the cave and stroking its tan fur. With a curse, Eamon came to his feet. "Out!"

"What—"

"It's a dingo!" He staggered up, falling against the cave wall. If that cub's mother was nearby, as it most certainly was, it would rip their throats out to protect her pup, violating their typical human avoidance. "Out! Now!"

A warning howl filled the night and drifted to the cave.

"Go go go," Eamon pushed her.

"But—"

He tripped. Went down—plunged into darkness. Fell.

"Eamon!" Ellis's scream followed him down the slope. Agony tore through Eamon as he rolled, pitched, and landed hard. The steepness increasing his momentum.

He flopped on his back and he shuffled with his feet to slow his descent. When he finally came to a stop, he arched his back. "Auuugh!"

Click.

Eamon froze at the sound of a chambering weapon.

CHAPTER 17

Eamon stared up into the muzzle of a M4. Cursed the risk they'd taken.

"Had enough fun yet?" Niehauer asked as he glowered at Eamon. "You've given us quite the chase, Corporal Straider, but setting off that beacon." He clicked his tongue. "It was almost like cheating."

Panting and grunting through the pain, Eamon considered his options. Wondered where—

"Come on down, Princess," Niehauer motioned up the steep drop Eamon had discovered. "You can die together."

His vision swam in and out. His hearing raced his vision to escape Eamon's grasp. The world swirled. Tilted.

"He's already dying," Ellis said. "You don't need a bullet to do it."

"You mean another bullet," Niehauer said, sneering at Eamon on the ground. "It's fitting, Beast of Cape York, that you die like the wild dogs of Australia. With them, even." He lifted the weapon and fired at something.

A yelp snapped through the night.

Eamon clenched his teeth. The knife in his boot . . . but he had no strength. Couldn't . . . couldn't even reach it. "Let her go."

"That is not going to happen and you know it."

Heaving through the pain and breaths, Eamon reached to a God he hadn't talked to in years. *Please . . . help us.* He didn't want them to hurt, maim, or do other horrible things to Ellis.

When she dropped to his side, he hooked an arm around her neck, though the move alone made him want to die. He glowered at Niehauer. A challenge set in his eyes.

"As you insist," Niehauer said, hefting the weapon again. "For Cory."

Eamon pressed his face into Ellis's hair and neck, felt her trembling. Knew it'd be over. Against her ear, he pressed a kiss. Whispered, "I'm sor—"

Crack!
Crack-crack-Pop!
Thud. Thump.
Crack. Thwat-thwat-thwat!

The fireworks reverberated through his chest. Pain. He should feel an explosion of pain. Or nothing. But . . . nothing.

"Y'all need a room or something?"

"Quiet, Cell."

Eamon lifted his head, disbelief spearing him as four men emerged in black tac gear and M4s.

Thor jogged toward Eamon and went to a knee, digging in a med pack. "Titanis. You okay?" He threaded a wide-bore needle into his arm. "Talk to me, Titanis."

"Aerial One, this is Wallaby Two. You're clear for approach."

A chopper. They were bringing in a chopper. "'Bout time you showed up." Throwing his head back, he fought the urge to cry. Fought he urge to howl through the pain. Instead, he simply clung to the only hope of a life he had—Ellis. Feeling the swirl of drugs rushing through his veins, he muttered, "Keep her safe."

Thor gave Ellis an appraising look. "Will do, Titanis." As he worked, the thunder of a helo grew louder, prying Eamon back to the bright afternoon. Thor hunched over him to protect him from whipping wind and dirt as the helo descended.

Half out of it, he startled when four men lifted him onto a

stretcher.

Ellis was there as they secured the stretcher onto the helo. "You did it again," she said, her mouth against his ear as she shouted. "You rescued me."

"You rescued *me*." Knowing his men would take care of her, Eamon released the death-grip on consciousness.

EPILOGUE

Six Months Later – ViCross II

THE VIEW HAD always been one he'd appreciated, staring out over the expanse of stress-free waters and undulating waves. Only now, there was a new, curvier view to appreciate. Wearing one of those long, clingy stretchy dresses in a shade of blue that matched the ocean behind her, Ellis stood at the starboard rail, staring into the distance. Her long reddish-blonde hair tangled on the wind, taunting his fingers to dig in.

Eamon strode up behind her and slipped his arm around her waist, drawing her back against his chest.

"Mm," she said relaxing and closing her eyes. She lifted her hand and reached back, cupping his face. "We deserve this vacation. Now that the veterans' complex is successfully under way, we can celebrate in style. Maybe we can fly to New York."

"What? My yacht isn't enough?"

She laughed. "It's more than enough, though I can't believe you got another one."

"Why, didn't think I had enough money?"

Another laugh. This one nearly caustic. "You forget—I'm Vic Toriael. I have intimate knowledge of your accounts."

"Intimate, eh?" He bent and pressed his lips to the sweet spot behind her ear—the one he knew drove her crazy. When she laughed and turned toward him, Eamon pulled her close and into a deep, long kiss. Tasting her sweetness, determining that this was the right decision for him.

"Whoa, Beast," she said, blushing even still. Her gaze skipped over his shoulder. She straightened, her crimson stain telling that she'd seen the witnesses. "We aren't alone."

"We shouldn't be."

Ellis straightened, her smile gone. Gaze bouncing to the guests. She gasped. "My parents."

Eamon kissed her again, taking his time. Lingering. Teasing. Easing the ring from his pocket. When he drew back, he made as if he'd thread their fingers together and instead, slipped the ring on her finger.

With a quick intake of breath, she pulled back.

Eamon grinned.

Her face was inscrutable. Had he misread her or what they'd shared since the *ViC I* went down?

"What's wrong?"

She wagged the homing-beacon of a ring. "Aren't you supposed to *ask* something?"

This—this was why he'd surrendered to her. "Going to make me beg?"

"Oh, for pity's sake," his mum said. "Do it right, Eamon."

He rolled his eyes, then considered the woman in his arms. Considered what they'd been through. "You were taken from me once. I don't want that to happen again. Ever. Will you—"

"Yes."

He arched an eyebrow.

"Begging doesn't become the Beast of Cape York."

ABOUT THE AUTHOR

Ronie Kendig is an award-winning, bestselling author who grew up an Army brat. She married a veteran, and together their lives are never dull with four children and a retired military working dog. Ronie's degree in Psychology has helped her pen novels of intense, raw characters.

Want to learn more about Ronie Kendig, visit her online!
Website: www.roniekendig.com
Facebook (facebook.com/rapidfirefiction)
Twitter (@roniekendig)
Goodreads (www.goodreads.com/RonieK)
Instagram (@kendigronie)
Pinterest (pinterest.com/roniek)

MORE RAPID-FIRE FICTION FROM RONIE KENDIG

THE QUIET PROFESSIONALS

Raptor 6
QUIET PROFESSIONALS #1

Captain Dean Watters keeps his mission and his team in the forefront of his laser-like focus. So when Dean's mission and team are threatened, his Special Forces training kicks into high gear. Failing to stop hackers from stealing national security secrets from the military's secure computers and networks isn't an option.

Hawk
QUIET PROFESSIONALS #2

Raptor's communications expert, Staff Sergeant Brian "Hawk" Bledsoe, is struggling with his inner demons, leaving him on the verge of an "other than honorable" discharge. Plagued with corrupted intel, Raptor team continues to track down the terrorist playing chess with their lives.

Falcon
QUIET PROFESSIONALS #3

Special Forces operator Salvatore "Falcon" Russo vowed to never again speak to or trust Lieutenant Cassandra Walker after a tragedy four years ago. But as Raptor closes in on the cyber terrorists responsible for killing two of their own, Sal must put his life—and the lives of his teammates—in her hands.

THE TOX FILES

The Warrior's Seal
THE TOX FILES prequel novella

Special Forces operative Cole "Tox" Russell and his team are tasked in a search-and-rescue—the U.S. president has been kidnapped during a goodwill tour. The mission nosedives when an ancient biblical artifact and a deadly toxin wipe out villages. Tox must stop the terrorists and the toxin to save the president.

Conspiracy of Silence
THE TOX FILES #1

Four years after a tragic mission decimated his career and his team, Cole "Tox" Russell is *persona non grata* to the United States. And that's fine—he just wants to be left alone. But when a dormant, centuries-old disease is unleashed, Tox is lured back into action.

Crown of Souls
THE TOX FILES #2, releasing September, 2017

Six months after stopping a deadly plague, Cole "Tox" Russell and his team are enjoying a little rest. That peace is short-lived when Tox is hit by a sniper shot. The enemy is one of their own, a rogue Special Forces team operator.

THE DISCARDED HEROES

Nightshade
DISCARDED HEROES #1

After a tour of duty in a war-torn country, embattled former Navy SEAL Max Jacobs finds himself discarded and alienated from those he loves as he struggles with combat-related PTSD.

Digitalis
DISCARDED HEROES #2

Colton Neeley left his military career to take care of his four-year old daughter. Although he's firm in his faith now, the repercussions of his former life are still evident—namely in the form of his daughter and his debilitating flashbacks from combat-related trauma.

Wolfsbane
DISCARDED HEROES #3

Haunted by memories of a mission gone bad, former Green Beret Canyon Metcalfe wrestles with misgivings and growing feelings for a senator's daughter embroiled in a nightmare. Setting aside his hesitation, he and Nightshade unravel lethal secrets.

Firethorn
DISCARDED HEROES #4

Former Marine and current Nightshade team member Griffin "Legend" Riddell is comfortable. So comfortable he never sees the set up that lands him in a maximum security prison, charged with murder. How can he prove his innocence behind bars?

A BREED APART

Trinity: Military War Dog
A BREED APART #1

A year ago in Afghanistan, Green Beret Heath Daniel's career was destroyed. Along with his faith. Now he and his military war dog, Trinity train other dogs and their handlers through the A Breed Apart organization. The job works. But his passion is to be back in the field.

Talon: Combat Tracking Team
A BREED APART #2

All Air Force veteran Aspen Courtland wants is her brother back. The US Marine Corps says he's dead, but Aspen won't believe it till she sees his body. Her only hope is her brother's tracking dog, Talon, but a brutal attack has left the dog afraid of his own shadow.

Beowulf: Explosives Detection Dog
A BREED APART #3

Former Navy handler Timbrel Hogan has more attitude than her Explosives Detection Dog, Beowulf, but she's a tough woman who gets the job done. Green Beret Tony "Candyman" VanAllen likes a challenge and convincing the hard-hitting handler they belong together might just get him killed. When tragedy strikes and Tony's career is jeopardized, Timbrel must re-evaluate her life and priorities—and fast.

OPERATION ZULU REDEMPTION

Operation Zulu Redemption

They never should've existed. Now they don't.

In the aftermath of their first highly successful op, the first all-female special ops team, known as Zulu, discovered that innocent civilians—women and children—died at their hands. Zulu was set up to take the devastating fall. Fearing for their lives, the Zulu team vanished.

DEAD RECKONING

Dead Reckoning

A Rapid-Fire Rewrite–Expanded & Updated–14,000 new words!

A deadly encounter in the Arabian Sea becomes a fight for her life!

Underwater archaeologist Shiloh Blake finds herself in the middle of an international nuclear arms clash during her first large-scale dig and flees for her life. She doesn't know who to trust or how to stay alive.

Want the latest Rapid-Fire intel on upcoming releases and events? Then become a recruit and join up. Start with my newsletter, then track me down on social media: Goodreads, Facebook, Instagram, and Twitter!

Excitement is contagious! The more reviews a book has, the more likely other readers are to find it. Please consider posting a review or rating to help Rapid-Fire Fiction gain a louder voice and audience.

Made in the USA
Middletown, DE
23 April 2018